SLAUGHTER

James Stewart

Published by

**MELROSE
  BOOKS**

An Imprint of Melrose Press Limited
St Thomas Place, Ely
Cambridgeshire
CB7 4GG, UK
www.melrosebooks.co.uk

FIRST EDITION

Copyright © James Stewart 2018

The Author asserts his moral right to
be identified as the author of this work

Cover by Melrose Books

**ISBN   978-1-912640-06-5 paperback
            978-1-912640-07-2 epub
            978-1-912640-08-9 mobi**

Printed and bound in Great Britain by:
Ashford Colour Press Ltd
Unit 600
Fareham Reach
Fareham Road
Gosport
PO13 0FW

Chapter 1

Ian and Richard Weatherhead, a father and son team, were slowly dismantling the marquee. Ian always thought it was such a pity to pull down a marquee only days after they'd put it up. It made him think of a jigsaw puzzle, hours spent achieving a beautiful picture only to trash it soon after completion.

This marquee was top quality. It had candy-striped awnings, Perspex windows all the way around and big French doors at the entrance. Inside, there had been chairs with white covers and pink bows and, on each table, pink candles and two foot high vases filled with pink and white flowers. A huge olive tree in an enormous pot stood in the centre of the marquee. Grand, decorative chandeliers provided the light.

It must have cost a pretty penny, thought Ian, although it now had that *morning after* feeling as only a few tables, chairs, stained tablecloths, empty and half-empty bottles and dirty glasses remained.

The house itself was classically beautiful, with acres of lawn to the side, upon which the marquee stood. *What a wedding this must have been,* thought Ian.

They were inside the marquee, beginning to dismantle the interior. The lights first and then the linings. They were chatting about the Yorkshire cricket match that had taken place that weekend: 'They haven't had a particularly good season so far, but it doesn't end 'til late September,' said Ian. 'Maybe Yorkshire'll win at the Scarborough Cricket Festival.'

'They've got some good lads coming on,' said Richard. 'Joe Root, David Bairstow's son, Jonny Bairstow, in the Academy doing well. Also, a foreigner called Gary Ballance from South

Africa, so I'm told.'

Just as they were chatting whilst working, a girl appeared at the entrance to the marquee by the open French doors. She was as white as a sheet and looked to be in a state of shock. She was sobbing uncontrollably into a napkin of some sort which she held to her face. She appeared to be wearing a white nightdress but nothing on her feet.

Ian stopped what he was doing and walked towards her: 'Anything we can do to help, lass?' he asked.

She could hardly speak. 'It's my family,' she sobbed. 'They've all been murdered and he raped me.' She was sobbing and mumbling so much that Ian could hardly pick up what she was saying.

'Come and sit yourself down, lass,' said Richard as he pulled a chair out from one of the tables. 'Tell us all about it, take your time.'

'They're all dead in the house,' she sobbed.

'Who's dead?'

'My Mummy and Daddy and David, my brother,' she mumbled as she wiped her eyes.

'Who on earth would do something like that, lass?' asked Ian.

'He gave a name, Jason somebody.'

'Richard, go and have a look, will you?' said Ian. 'Is the house open, lass?'

'Yes,' she said.

Richard left and came back a few minutes later. 'It's true,' he said as he rushed outside the marquee to vomit.

'I'll ring the police,' said Ian.

Clouds moved above the marquee, blocking the sun, as if bowing in sympathy.

Chapter 2

DCI James Turnbull was in his office at the Bradford Police Headquarters, looking out of the window at the Bradford Alhambra across the road. His thoughts drifted back to the early days when, as a child, he'd seen Les Dawson in pantomime. His dad used to tell him about the stars of the past; Albert Modley, Nat Jackley, Gracie Fields, Max Bygraves. James had taken his wife, Helen, there recently to see The Bachelors, who she loved, even though they were getting a bit past it.

Just as he was thinking, his telephone rang: 'Sir, we've got a triple murder in Ilkley. A posh house beyond Nesfield. It sounds horrific.'

'What's the address?' Turnbull asked as he picked up a pen and grabbed a piece of paper. 'And the postcode?'

'The Hollins, LS29 0BQ.'

'I'm on my way. Find Dave Jasper. Tell him it's urgent and get him to meet me at my car. I assume uniform are there.'

'Yes, sir, they're at the house. I'll page Dave Jasper now.'

James grabbed his Mac, just in case it rained, and walked quickly down the long corridor to the stairs. DS Dave Jasper caught him up.

'What's happened?' he asked.

'A triple murder, apparently. Get the team there and warn uniform we may need a search party. We need immediately, a cameraman, a police surgeon, a pathologist, SOCO and photographer. It's at a house called The Hollins in Nesfield, Ilkley. The postcode's LS29 0BQ.

'Will do,' said Dave, using his mobile whilst rushing down the stairs with Turnbull.

They blue-lighted out of Bradford to Shipley, Guiseley, Menston and Ilkley, passing Ilkley Golf Club on their way to Nesfield.

'Posh area,' said Dave.

'The best. Colin Montgomery used to play here,' said Turnbull pointing towards the golf course which meandered along the side of the river Wharfe. 'That tells you a thing or two.'

"The Hollins" had a gated entrance with a lodge at the gate. *That must be for the staff* thought Turnbull. He pressed the button on the intercom and announced who he was. The gate slowly opened. They drove up a long, winding drive with mature rhododendrons on each side. *What a pad* thought Turnbull.

They reached the house which was fronted by a sweeping driveway surrounding a water fountain. *That's some turning circle* thought Jasper who'd never been to such a magnificent house. Two police cars were already parked there.

A stone porch, with round pillars on each side and a sloping slate roof, led to the main door. A carved stone plaque announced that the house was built in 1823. Turnbull rang the doorbell which was immediately answered by a uniformed PC.

He didn't recognise the PC, but the PC recognised him: 'Sir, we were first here after a 999 call from the marquee contractor. The deceased are Gordon Hodges and his wife, Amelia Hodges, also their son, David Hodges. One's on the stairs and the other two are in separate bedrooms upstairs. The daughter, Amy Hodges, is sitting in the marquee with a policewoman. She looks shattered and she says she's been raped.'

'Thanks,' said Turnbull as he and Jasper entered the house.

From the huge entrance hall, a wide, sweeping staircase led to the first floor. On the stairs, Turnbull saw the body of a silver-haired man wearing a morning suit. He looked, to Turnbull, as though he'd been stabbed. His shirt and waistcoat, covering his chest, were soaked in blood. Turnbull checked for a pulse. There was no pulse and no doubt that he was dead.

In one bedroom, on the first floor, they found a young man lying on the bed. Turnbull presumed this was David Hodges. He was wearing morning suit trousers, but not the jacket or waistcoat. His throat had been cut and he, too, had no pulse and was dead.

In the adjacent bedroom, they found Amelia Hodges, a middle-aged woman, wearing a dressing-gown. She was lying on the floor and she too appeared to have been stabbed in the chest. She didn't have a pulse and there was no doubt that she also was dead.

Turnbull and Jasper went back downstairs and out of the front door. They were glad to breathe in some fresh air as they walked round the house and across the lawn and into the marquee by a side door. Sitting there, with her head bowed, was a young woman whom Turnbull assumed was Amy Hodges. Next to her was a uniformed policewoman who was attempting, unsuccessfully, to comfort her.

Amy looked about nineteen, with short hair in a simple style with a fringe over her forehead. She was somewhat dishevelled and her right foot looked to be caked in blood which had been seeping between her toes. She was wearing a full length, blood-stained white nightdress.

Turnbull and Jasper pulled up a chair each to sit near her and the marquee contractors stood to the side.

'Hello, love, I'm DCI James Turnbull and this is DS Dave Jasper. What's your name?'

'Amy Hodges.'

'Well, Amy, we know you'll want us to catch the person

responsible as soon as we can so, if you feel up to it, we'd like you to tell us what happened.'

'Yes, I understand that,' said Amy. 'God, what a nightmare. What have we done to deserve this? The slaughter of a good family. I'll help you all I can and tell you all I know. Can I have some water, please?'

'Of course,' said Turnbull as the policewoman went to get her a glass of water from the house. 'First of all, did you see who did it?'

'Yes, I did,' she said. 'He said his name was Jason.'

'Can you tell us, love, whether he touched anything? Try to reconstruct in your mind everything that happened and concentrate on whether he touched anything,' said Turnbull.

'Well, he drank from one of those half empty bottles of champagne over there. Presumably the caterers left them because they weren't finished.'

'Please show us.'

Amy led them to some half-drunk bottles on a trestle table. 'I think, in fact I'm sure, it was this one. He drank from the bottle,' she said as she pointed to a bottle at the edge of the table. Dave put on some rubber gloves, picked up the bottle and placed it in an exhibits bag.

'He wasn't wearing any gloves then?' asked Turnbull.

'No.'

'Okay, did he touch anything else?'

'Yes, he took me into the kitchen and he helped himself to some cheese from the fridge.'

'Show us, please,' said Turnbull.

They accompanied Amy out of the marquee, down the tented passageway, to the house where they walked through double doors, down the hall and into a beautifully appointed kitchen. Amy identified the fridge and the cheese which Dave carefully placed in a separate exhibits bag.

'Make sure that's refrigerated ASAP,' said Turnbull.

'Will do,' replied Dave. 'In fact, I'll leave it in the fridge until SOCO arrive.'

'Well done, Amy,' said Turnbull. 'Is there anything else like that that you can remember?'

'He was bleeding from a cut on his leg and some of the blood got on my nightie,' she replied as she pointed to the bloodstain.

'Okay, Amy,' said Turnbull. 'We're going to have to take your nightgown as evidence. We need it straight away, so please will you go with the policewoman and take it off and give it to her. You can get changed into something else, but please don't have a shower at the moment.'

'Yes, I'll do that. Do you want me to go now?'

'Yes, please, but remember that you mustn't wash your hands or any part of your body. We are awaiting the police surgeon and the pathologist, Professor John Talbot. They will be here any minute. One of them, probably the police surgeon, will examine you in the presence of this policewoman. Is that okay?'

'Yes,' replied Amy in a dull, almost monotone, voice.

'The pathologist will also examine your mum, dad and brother and then they'll be taken away. Meanwhile, the SOCO team, that's Scenes of Crime Officers, are here. They're led by Bill Thornton and he'll need to have a word with you. Can you tell us whether you think the man touched anything else?'

'No, I don't think so.'

'How did he get into the house?' asked Turnbull.

'I don't know.'

'Fair enough, something may come to you whilst we ask you questions and we can always revisit what else he may have touched, or how he got in, a bit later,' said Turnbull.

'Let's start at the beginning, shall we?' said Turnbull. 'We'll break off when the police surgeon and pathologist arrive.

'Now, about the wedding, whose was it?'

'Jane's. She's my elder sister. She married George Waterhouse yesterday afternoon.'

'That was the 26th of September?'

'Yes, it was.'

'What time did it finish?' asked Turnbull.

'About eight o'clock.'

'And then what?

'Mummy, Daddy and David went to my aunt and uncle's house for supper. I didn't want to go, I felt tired and my feet were killing me. It had been a long day. They left here about nine o'clock.'

'What did you do?' asked Turnbull.

'I made a few phone calls to friends and then I had a shower and went to bed about ten o'clock.'

'Then what?'

'I was woken up by Mummy's screaming. I don't know what time it was. I think the screaming was coming from her bedroom. Then I heard two men's voices outside my bedroom. One was Daddy's. He was shrieking and shouting. There were bangs and sounds of choking. I thought I was having a nightmare.

'Then I heard Mummy shouting *"Take all the money, anything, just go and leave us alone"* and then she screamed some more. I was terrified and daren't get out of bed. I was just curled up, like a foetus, trembling.'

'There, there, love,' said Turnbull. 'Now then, Professor Talbot and the police surgeon have just arrived. Will you go now, be examined, have a shower and maybe something to eat, and then we'll carry on. Okay? The police surgeon will take a swab from your right foot and probably your private parts. They've had to do this sort of thing many times, so they'll be very gentle with you. Okay?'

'Yes, thank you, you're very kind,' said Amy as she left the marquee with the policewoman.

'What do you think?' asked Jasper.

'Well, whoever did this is a bloody maniac, that's for sure. What can possibly have been the point, the reason for all this?'

'Search me,' said Jasper.

Turnbull went out of the marquee for some fresh air. It was a beautiful late summer's day. He'd never seen a marquee like it. It stood majestically on the manicured lawn which had recently been cut in totally straight, wide stripes. *Looks just like the grass at Wimbledon*, he thought. Mature oak trees surrounded the huge lawn.

The Hollins stood high on the hillside of Middleton, the side of the valley which caught the sun for most of the day. He stood for a moment to take in the beautiful view before him. He could see the Cow and Calf Rocks in the distance, on the edge of Ilkley Moor, on the opposite side of the valley. The river Wharfe meandered its way through the bottom of the valley.

Turnbull sometimes came to Ilkley with his wife, Helen, to enjoy a walk along the riverside and then spoil themselves with a visit to Betty's Tearooms for their famous afternoon teas.

To the south, Turnbull knew that the landscape changed, giving way to moorland, majestic mill chimneys and narrow winding streets which, in bygone eras, housed weavers and mill-workers. Such mills had long since closed and been converted into fashionable flats, gift shops and pubs.

Turnbull got on his mobile and rang headquarters. 'Anything

I should know?' he asked.

'Well, sir, there was an escape from custody at Keighley and Bingley Magistrates' Court four days ago at about 2:30 pm. The escapee's name is Arthur Mallinson. He was due to appear for a committal hearing at the Magistrates' Court for burglary of a dwelling house on Park Road, Bingley. He has no form and, for some reason, we don't have a photograph of him taken after his arrest.

'There's been a hunt out for him since the 22nd, but, so far, he's avoided detection. The manhunt was limited in extent as he was only up for burglary.'

'He could be our guy,' said Turnbull. 'Keep me informed.'

'Will do. How are things at your end?'

'We're interviewing a very plucky young girl whose mum, dad and brother have been murdered. She's only nineteen and it looks as though she's been raped. Can you find the police artist? We need him here ASAP, especially as there's no photograph of this Arthur Mallinson.'

'Will do. Anything else?'

'No, thanks, not for the moment,' said Turnbull as he walked back into the marquee, where he found SOCO's Bill Thornton examining the champagne bottle.

'Any luck, Bill?' he asked.

'Yes, James, we've found two prints on the bottle. One at the neck where he probably handled it and a palm print on the bottle itself. The waiters, so I'm told by the marquee men who often work with them, were wearing white gloves, which is a blessing. It's surprising that our man wasn't wearing gloves.

'As for the cheese, matching bite marks is the job of the forensic odontologist. He'll need the suspect's dental records to have any chance, unless you get your man to bite some polyvinyl siloxane so we can get his teeth marks.'

10

Professor Talbot walked into the marquee with the police surgeon, Doctor John Carr.

Turnbull greeted them. 'Well, two Johns, good to see you again. The last time we met was in the *missing au pair* case.'

'And that was a turn up for the books,' said Talbot.

'Well, what've you got?' asked Turnbull.

'Marks on the girl's wrists, indicative of some sort of handcuffs or a struggle. There were seven transverse scratches on her left wrist, six by two centimetres, and four of similar dimensions on the right wrist.

'I've seen marks like this before when a person's been wearing handcuffs and trying to release themselves. They're fresh within the last ten hours. The skin is rucked up and bruised.'

'And her private parts?' queried Turnbull.

'No fresh injury. She complained of discomfort, but nothing to see. John's taken swabs but there's no obvious sign of semen. She'd blood caked on her right foot and we've taken a swab.'

'What about the murder victims?' asked Turnbull.

'Father repeatedly stabbed in the chest with a large knife. He'll have died very quickly.

'Mother also stabbed in the chest. She'll also have died very quickly.

'Son's throat cut whilst he was in bed. The same,' said Talbot.

'Can we arrange for the bodies to be taken away?' asked Turnbull.

'Yes,' said Talbot. 'Have them taken to the morgue and I'll carry out the post mortems tonight. I'll see you tomorrow with my report.'

Professor Talbot left the marquee but Doctor Carr, the police surgeon, remained in case Amy needed a sedative. 'She shouldn't be left alone,' he said.

Turnbull's mind turned to the dreadful ordeal this poor young girl had gone through. *What a bugger,* he thought; *spending hours with a man who'd raped her after murdering her immediate family, except for her sister who'd just got married and left home. Now she was alone. How dreadful.*

Ten minutes or so later, Amy returned to the marquee. She was wearing a tracksuit and her damp hair was combed back from her face. She was still sobbing. Doctor Carr approached her as she walked in with the policewoman. He told her he would stay with her for a while and she looked relieved to hear that.

Turnbull pulled up a chair for her. 'Amy, can you go to a relative's tonight? We don't want you to stay here.'

'Yes, I'm sure I can go to my aunt's. Can I ring her?' she asked.

'Yes, if you like or I'll do it for you,' replied Turnbull.

'No, I'll do it, thank you,' said Amy as she touched the screen of her mobile phone. Turnbull was sitting close enough to her to hear a voice answer.

'Aunt Violet, it's Amy, have you heard what's happened?'

'No, tell me.'

'It'll wait. I need you to come and collect me straight away. I'll tell you all about it when you get here. Can you come?'

'Of course, darling,' said Aunt Violet obviously realising it wise not to say anything else but to just go. She could sense the urgency.

'Right, Amy,' said Turnbull. 'Are you ready to continue?'

'Yes.'

'We'd reached the point where you thought you were having a nightmare when you heard your mum and dad shouting and screaming. What happened next?' asked Turnbull.

'Well, then someone came into my room. It was a man and he said *"Turn the light on"*. He sounded drunk, horrible. I switched on the bedside lamp. He came over to the bed, pulled back the duvet and put his hand on my right shoulder. He said *"Scream and you're dead"*.

'I could now see his face in the light. It was haggard, unshaven and dirty. He smelled of BO as though he hadn't washed for days. I wanted to vomit. It was disgusting. He had a knife in his left hand, a sort of sheath knife.'

'Would you be able to describe him to an artist?' asked Turnbull.

'Yes, I think so,' said Amy as more tears rolled down her cheeks.

'Are you alright to carry on?' asked Turnbull. 'I know it's hard for you.'

'Yes, I'm okay. He held the knife to my throat. I wanted to scream but nothing would come out. He said *"Get up"* and he made me walk downstairs, through the tented entrance and into the marquee. I didn't see Daddy on the stairs because there weren't any lights on, only the light from my bedroom, but I felt my foot brush against something and I stood in something wet.

'We entered the marquee. He told me to put the lights on. He then led me to the end of the marquee where he handcuffed my wrists in front of me. I don't know where he got the handcuffs from or the key for them. I didn't resist, I just pleaded with him not to kill me. He said he wouldn't as long as I did as I was told.

'He pushed me to the floor and lifted my nightie. I had nothing on underneath. He lowered his trousers and I could see that his leg was bleeding. He said he wanted to fuck me. He did. I don't know whether he came. I just didn't move.

I couldn't move because he was on top of me and he'd pushed my handcuffed arms above my head. I was so terrified. It hurt. I was dry.

'He dragged me up and walked me across the marquee. He drank some champagne from the bottle I showed you and then he walked me back to the house where he told me to show him where the kitchen was. Mummy had left the kitchen light on for when they came home. That's when he ate the cheese I showed you.

'Then he said *"We're going back upstairs"* and he walked me back to my bedroom.'

'So, you didn't resist when he said he was going to penetrate you?' asked Turnbull.

'No, I couldn't. I just lay there and let him do it. I was frozen with fear. I couldn't believe what was happening to me. It was a nightmare. He made me walk back upstairs and into my bedroom. Again, I stood in something wet on the stairs.

'He took the handcuffs off and then he pulled my nightie off. He started to talk to me as though I was his girlfriend. It was weird.

'He said he'd been on the run for several days. He said he was good at avoiding the police. He said the police had passed near him but they didn't see him.

'He said he'd been in the woods where he could see the marquee and watch the comings and goings. He said to call him Joe or Jason, I can't remember which. He had an accent. I thought it was Geordie, but I can't be sure. He kept saying his leg was bleeding.

'He pushed me onto the bed and raped me again. I don't know if he came. He kept talking for ages. I just lay there. I was terrified. I was sure he was going to kill me. I was so relieved when he left.'

'Do you know what time that was, Amy?' asked Turnbull.

'About 6:00 a.m.'

'I hesitate to ask you this, Amy, but are you taking any contraceptives?'

'No,' she replied.

'Please will you tell the doctor that?' asked Turnbull.

'Oh my God, do you think he might have made me pregnant?'

Amy let out a piercing howl and banged her fist on the table in frustration.

Turnbull let her recover her composure and said, 'I doubt it, but better be on the safe side.' After another pause, he asked, 'What happened after he left?'

'Yes, of course,' she replied.

'What happened after he left?' asked Turnbull.

'I cowered in bed until I heard the sound of a vehicle on the driveway. I got up and looked out of the window. It was the marquee men and the rest you know.'

'Thank you, Amy, you've done really well.'

Turnbull called over the police surgeon and explained about the lack of contraception. Doctor Carr said he would come back with a morning-after pill. Just as they were chatting, Max, the police artist, arrived. Turnbull explained the situation and took him over to introduce him to Amy.

'Amy, do you mind sitting with Max and describing the man's face and features?' asked Turnbull.

'No, I don't mind, I'll never forget that face. That revolting man: his face will haunt for the rest of my life,' she sobbed. 'Is Aunt Violet here yet?'

'Yes, she's waiting in the sitting-room. I've had to tell her what's happened. Obviously, she's distraught but she's being very strong and protective of you,' replied Turnbull. 'She's going to contact your sister and brother-in-law to tell them what's happened. I'm sure they'll want to come home to be with you.'

'Thank you,' said Amy.

Max pulled up a couple of chairs, placing his drawing pad and pencils on one of them: 'Hello, Amy,' he said.

'I'll leave you with Max,' said Turnbull. 'And then you can go with your aunt. Speak to Doctor Carr before you go, he'll be back shortly with a pill for you.

'What you've said will be reduced to a witness statement which you can see tomorrow. If it's accurate, please sign it. If there's anything you're not happy with, alter it and initial the alteration. One other thing, did he steal anything?'

'I don't know.'

'Can you remember anything else?'

'No.'

'Finally, how tall was he? Was he well built?'

'I'd say about six feet and about fourteen stones. He was strong and muscular.'

'And how old do you think he would be?'

'Far too old for me, probably in his forties or fifties. I can't say. I'm not very good at ages.'

'I'll see you again soon,' said Turnbull. 'Take care of yourself. Oh, did Doctor Carr give you a sleeping pill?'

'No, he said he would give it to my aunt when she arrived.'

'Ah, that's good. Bye for now Amy.'

'Bye and thanks Mr Turnbull.'

Turnbull and Jasper went outside to organise the search team. As they did so, they could see the police photographer video-ing the scene. *He won't like that,* thought Turnbull, *I've never seen a murder scene as bad as that in my entire career.*

Chapter 3

The three bodies were taken to the mortuary in the basement at St James's University Hospital in Leeds. The autopsy room, which was Professor Talbot's workplace, had white tiled walls. A stainless steel table, with gutters, stood in the centre of the room.

Professor Talbot carried out the post mortems and his findings were much as he had expected. He could tell that the murder weapon used on Gordon and Amelia Hodges was a single-bladed knife with a four-inch, sharp blade, probably a sheath or Bowie knife. It had penetrated the hearts of both victims. From the track of the wound, which was slightly inward, he assessed the thrust was right-handed and slightly upwards and would have caused almost instant death.

He could not tell what sort of knife had been used to cut David Hodges' throat save that it had a very sharp blade.

There were no illnesses apparent in any of the three victims which could have contributed to their deaths.

What a waste of three lives, and one so young, thought Talbot.

Chapter 4

Thirty policemen were gathered outside the house by their cars. They were all wearing their search gear: white tracksuits with police markings, police caps and walking boots. They all looked very professional and Turnbull was proud of them. He'd worked with them before. Theirs was an arduous and sometimes thankless task. Turnbull addressed them.

'Right lads, inside the house are three dead members of one family, slaughtered for God only knows what reason. The murderer, whose identity we don't yet know, is on the loose. He's got several hours start. We don't know where. He may be nearby, he may have left the area completely, but we have to check everything. The weapon he used was a Bowie or sheath knife. He may have discarded it, so keep your eyes open for it.

'Although we don't have a photograph of him, we'll shortly have an artist's impression. Max, the artist, is in the house with Amy. She's the daughter who survived. She's a bright young girl, nineteen years old, obviously severely traumatised by this dreadful ordeal and, what's more, she's been raped by the murderer. It won't be long before I'm able to give each of you a copy of the artist's impression.

'Meanwhile, from Amy's description of the man, I sense he's been living rough and so he's devious and streetwise. We think he may have stolen from the house but, at this stage, we're not sure. He may have bought a bus or train ticket, or even hitched a lift. He's fit, about fourteen stones and about six feet tall. He's unshaven and Amy said his leg was bleeding, so he may be limping. She said she thought he was called Joe or Jason and he had an accent. She thought it might have been a

Geordie accent, but she couldn't be sure.

'First of all, search the grounds and then fan out. If we get a sighting from elsewhere, we'll radio it to you and you can get to that area ASAP. You've got radios to keep in touch with each other. It's possible we'll need an armed response unit to take him. We know he's got, or at least he had, a knife. We have no evidence that he's got a gun, but we can't rule it out.

'Uniform are at the bus and railway stations in Ilkley and roadblocks have been set up on the Otley and Skipton roads out of Ilkley and on the moor road to Burley Woodhead.

'I know it's like looking for a needle in a haystack, but we have to do this just in case he or the weapon's nearby.

'Good luck. I'll be back at Bradford HQ keeping tabs on your movements. When Max has finished his drawing, he'll give each of you a copy. Fortunately, there's a photocopier in the house.'

Three uniformed officers were left guarding the house on the off-chance the killer might return. This man's movements are totally unpredictable.

Turnbull made sure that one of the officers would unite Amy with her aunt and see them safely off the premises and to her aunt's house.

Turnbull and Jasper returned to Bradford HQ. *It's now a waiting game,* thought Turnbull. His nose told him that if the killer had been living rough, he'd head north rather than into the urban areas of Shipley, Bradford or Leeds.

Soon, the artist's impression would be on local television, breaking into whatever programme was on at the time. It was to be shown every hour.

Meanwhile, Turnbull got DC Jane Rowley to check the artist's impression against mug-shots. Jasper was checking buses and trains. All Turnbull could do was wait.

Four hours later, he got a call from Keighley police station. It was the DCI there, a man called Lythe. Turnbull didn't know him.

'DCI Turnbull, I've just seen your artist's impression,' said Lythe.

'But it's been out for four hours,' said Turnbull. 'Didn't you see it when it was first released?'

'I'm afraid not. I've only just seen it,' said Lythe.

'Well, you bloody well should've seen it sooner. What do you know?'

'Well, I think it's a man who escaped from custody at our local Magistrate's Court four days ago. G4S were meant to be guarding him. He broke a window in the room he was being held in and climbed out. He's like an eel – slippery. He was due to appear for a committal to Bradford Crown Court for burglary of a dwelling house,' explained Lythe.

'What's his name? I hope at least you found that out,' said Turnbull feeling extremely irritated. 'The artist's impression would have had urgent plastered all over it in red.'

'There's no need to be sarcastic. Yes, his name is Arthur Mallinson. Nothing recorded against him,' replied Lythe.

'Did you take a photograph of him on his arrest?'

'I'm afraid we didn't, but your artist's impression is pretty good.'

'What sort of station do you run there, one for beginners?'

'Look, I'm sorry,' said Lythe. 'We just hadn't completed the formalities when he escaped. We've circulated details of his escape, but nothing so far.'

'Please keep me posted,' said Turnbull. *And thanks for nothing,* he thought as he rang off.

Turnbull looked at the large map of West Yorkshire pinned to the notice-board in his office and wondered where this man would go. How odd, a triple murderer with no previous form. He'd managed to stay out of sight from the search after his escape from the Magistrates' Court. He must be skilled at lying low. He hoped that all the usual checks had been carried out even though they were without success.

If he's used to living rough, thought Turnbull, *he would head north into the countryside of the North Yorkshire Dales, not south-east to the urban areas of Leeds, Bradford and Shipley. How far north would he have got by now if on foot? Masham area at most but, if he hitched a lift, even further. We should, if possible, check with people who know him to see if he's any favourite haunts.*

He called Jane Rowley into his office. Jane had recently joined the Murder Squad from the fast track. She was twenty-nine, unmarried and a highly intelligent officer.

'Hi, Jane. You know our man's details. Try and find his mother and father and see if they've heard from him, or know where he might have gone,' said Turnbull.

'Yes, sir, will do,' she replied.

* * *

Jane was the computer expert in the team. In Jane's opinion, James Turnbull was a bit of a philistine when it came to computers. She greatly enjoyed being a member of the Murder Squad. She was learning every day from Turnbull and Dave Jasper. However, work hours meant that she had no social life or boyfriend. After two unsuccessful incidents when dating police officers, she was determined to find someone outside the force. However, now was the time to prove her worth as a member of the squad.

First, she checked whether Mallinson was on the police

computer as having a criminal record. Nothing was shown.

She rang the local councils to see whether they had a Mallinson on their records. Bradford Metropolitan Council came up with three Mallinsons. Jane explained that Arthur Mallinson was in his forties or fifties and may have lived with his parents in the past.

'Well,' said the council worker, 'we have a Geoffrey and Deirdre Mallinson in Shipley and they have three voters in the house. The two of them and the third is registered as Arthur.'

'That'll be our man,' said Jane. 'Please could you give me the address?'

'Yes, it's 42 Poplar Crescent, Shipley.'

'Thank you for your help,' said Jane as she gathered her things together. She made her way down to the car park and set off to find the Mallinsons' house. It wasn't far from Bradford HQ to the address in Shipley, but it was a slow journey, creeping along Canal Road. One of Bradford's problems was its road system.

The Mallinsons' home was a terrace house near Salts Mill, which was now a World Heritage site and housed the biggest collection of David Hockney's works of art in the world. Hockney had a strong association with Bradford, having attended Bradford Boys' Grammar School, one of the best schools in the country in Hockney's day. It was now co-ed and renamed Bradford Grammar School. Jane wished it had been co-ed when she was of school age. She had been to a Catholic school called St Joseph's College in Manningham, Bradford.

She drew up in front of the house after managing, with some difficulty, to find a parking place. She put a police notice on the inside of the windscreen just in case she exceeded the time allowed. She approached the front door and rang the bell which was answered in no time by a lady in her early seventies.

She was skinny with a pronounced stoop. She wore an apron and looked as if Jane had caught her in the middle of baking.

'Hello, I'm Detective Jane Rowley from the Bradford police. We are looking for Arthur Mallinson. Could he be your son?'

'Oh, not again,' said the woman. 'Yes, I'm Deirdre, his mum. Come in lass. Geoff,' she shouted as she ushered Jane into the porch.

A lame, fat, elderly man came slowly down the stairs with the aid of his walking stick. He was clean-shaven and was wearing a loose cardigan and braces to hold up his trousers. 'What's up now?' he asked.

'This young lady is from the police and she's looking for our Arthur. Detective, this is Geoff, Arthur's dad.'

Geoff nodded at Jane and the three of them went into the front parlour which was neat and tidy, but hot and stuffy with no windows open. *Fancy wearing a cardigan in this heat. Let's hope this doesn't take long,* thought Jane as they sat down.

'First, let me show you an artist's impression,' said Jane as she pulled the sketch out of her briefcase.

'My God, that's a good likeness of our Arthur, but he's normally particular about his appearance and wouldn't have stubble. But that's him alright,' said Deirdre.

'How old is your son?' asked Jane.

'Geoff, how old will our Arthur be?'

'Forty-five next,' replied Geoff. 'What's he been up to this time?'

Jane thought the remark somewhat surprising as Mallinson didn't have a criminal record.

'Haven't you seen this impression on TV?' asked Jane.

'No,' said Geoff. 'We don't watch much TV. Too left wing for our liking.'

'Well, there's no easy way of telling you this, but we suspect he's committed murder.'

'Oh, my God,' said Deirdre. 'That's not like our Arthur, is it Geoff? It can't be him. It must be a mistake. Well, I don't know lass. I suppose the sooner he's found, the sooner the mistake can be dealt with.'

'When did you last see him?' asked Jane.

'About three weeks ago. He dropped in. A family man is our Arthur.'

Not much of a family man, thought Jane, *if it's three weeks since you've seen him.*

'Was he here long?'

'About an hour. He said he was just passing. He had some tea and then left.'

'Did he say what he was doing now?'

'He said he was looking for work. Good with his hands is our Arthur. He's never settled down since he left the army.'

That's interesting, thought Jane. *An army man would be good at lying low.*

'We think he's on the run,' said Jane. 'It's in his best interests that we find him. Have you any idea where he might have gone? Has he any particular haunts?'

'Well, we used to go on our holidays to a farm in North Yorkshire, near Middleham it was. Nice people who had some static caravans. He used to love it there. I've got the address somewhere,' said Geoff.

'It's in the dresser in our telephone book,' said Deirdre.

Geoff went searching.

'Ah, yes, here it is,' said Geoff. 'Graveley Hall Farm, near Middleham. Horse country. Arthur used to love the horses.'

'Does he like the countryside?' asked Jane.

'Oh, yes, he loved camping and shooting rabbits with his air pistol and then skinning them and cooking them,' said Deirdre.

'Can you think of anywhere else he might have gone?' asked Jane.

'No, not off hand,' said Deirdre.

'Does he have an accent?' asked Jane.

'Oh, yes,' replied Deirdre. 'Yorkshire like us.'

'Does he sound a bit Geordie?'

'Well, he did spend a long time in North Yorkshire. Their accent is different to West Yorkshire.'

'Well, thanks,' said Jane. 'You've been very helpful. Here's my card, please ring me any time if you think of anything which may help us find him, and especially if he gets in touch with you.'

'Will do,' they said in unison as Jane left, relieved to get out into the fresh air.

Chapter 5

Dave Jasper had the job of circulating information about Arthur Mallinson to the media and making sure the artist's impression was widely circulated to the general public. Jane's information about Arthur Mallinson coincided with Turnbull's hunch that he may have headed north.

Dave was also responsible for chasing up a forensic odontologist to look at the teeth marks left on the cheese. Dave found one, a Professor Hughes, from the Law Society's list of experts and, as luck would have it, he was based at Leeds University. Dave spoke to him to ask for his assistance.

'Well, if you can get the dental records,' replied Professor Hughes. 'I'll have a go. It would be better if you could get your suspect to bite on a substance we use for these purposes. It's like putty, but it's not degradable and it leaves an exact impression. Dentists use it in preparation for fitting crowns.'

'Okay. When and if we arrest him, we'll ask him to do that. Would you need to be there when he does it?' asked Dave.

'Ideally, yes, and then I can bring the substance with me. It may take more than one bite.'

'Thanks,' said Dave. 'We'll be in touch.'

Dave's next job was to chase up the forensic evidence. He spoke to Bill Thornton at the Home Office Laboratory in Wetherby. After exchanging pleasantries, he asked him how he was progressing.

'Well, the bloodstains on the nightdress differ. The one on the front is a rare blood group. One in fifty thousand has it. Whether or not it's your man's I just don't know because he's not on our database.

'The bloodstain on the neck of the nightdress matches the girl's mother's group. It's a fairly common group, but DNA tests confirm that it's highly likely to be her mother's. As for the blood sample from the girl's foot, that's different, but it's the same blood group as her father's.

'Then we come to the fingerprints on the champagne bottle. They have at least sixteen ridge characteristics which, as you know, are the criteria used for admissibility of fingerprint evidence in court. In fact, there are over thirty ridge characteristics. So, we must get your man's fingerprints as soon as he's arrested, then we'll know whether or not he held the champagne bottle.

'I'll submit my report in the next twenty-four hours.'

'Thanks for that, Bill. I'll let you know as soon as we get the guy,' said Dave. He put down the phone and reported Bill's findings to James Turnbull.

Chapter 6

The following morning, James Turnbull was at HQ awaiting news of sightings of the suspect after the artist's impression had been televised and distributed widely. He was now sure that the killer/rapist was Arthur Mallinson, who was clearly very dangerous.

What possible motive could he have had for these senseless killings? thought Turnbull. *At his trial, he'd probably try to raise a defence of diminished responsibility, reducing what otherwise would be murder to manslaughter. Whether that would succeed would depend on whether a psychiatrist would be prepared to say Mallinson, at the time of the killings, suffered from an abnormality of mind, in the medical sense. If not, he was surely doomed. But even if that defence succeeded, he surely would be locked away for life in a prison or mental institution such as Broadmoor.*

Turnbull sat back in his chair, chewing the top of his pen. *I'm surprised,* he pondered. *That at forty-five, Mallinson doesn't have a criminal record. Maybe he'd been so good at covering his tracks he hadn't been caught.*

Now that he thought about it, Turnbull decided it was time to investigate unsolved murders. He would get Jane Rowley on to that when she had a moment.

His telephone rang; it was DS Roberts who was responsible for the team taking calls in response to the media coverage.

'We've had the usual crackpots,' he said, 'but one looks interesting. A green-keeper at Masham Golf Club rang in just now. They have a rain shelter on the fourth hole and, at six o'clock this morning, he disturbed a man who was sleeping in it. He said he immediately saw a resemblance between him and the artist's impression he'd seen on the TV. Fortunately, the man didn't cause a scene; he just apologised and walked off. That was three hours ago. God only knows why the green-keeper waited until now to ring us. Oh, and he said he thought he saw what looked like a gun, but he couldn't be sure.'

'Well,' said Turnbull. 'Tell the armed response unit to get over there and fan out. I'll get up there in a helicopter. I'm setting off now for the airport. We've a better chance of spotting him from the air. Fortunately, it's a clear day.'

Turnbull and Jasper set off post-haste for Leeds/Bradford Airport. With the blue light flashing, they were at the airport and in the helicopter within half an hour. They'd called in advance and were lucky there was a helicopter available and it was ready and waiting for them. They knew the pilot, George Wood, as he'd flown them on many occasions in the past.

'Morning, George,' said Turnbull as he and Jasper climbed aboard and strapped themselves in. 'Thanks for your assistance. Our man was seen, we think, at Masham Golf Club about three and a half hours ago.'

'Well, visibility is good,' said George. 'No cloud cover. We'll be there shortly.'

They set off from what Turnbull remembered as Yeadon Airport and flew north to Nidderdale. As they flew up the valley, they had a clear view of Otley and Ilkley to the west and then the Yorkshire Dales National Park. Turnbull pointed out Nesfield where the murders had taken place. To the east they could see Harrogate, Boroughbridge and Ripon. By road it would have been a journey of some thirty miles and would have taken them the best part of two hours but, in no time at all, George was hovering over the golf course.

The course had been cleared and closed by order of the

police. George hovered for a minute until they could see the shelter in which it was thought Mallinson had slept. 'There it is,' said Turnbull. 'You can see where the local police have taped the area off.'

They hovered, keeping their eyes peeled whilst waiting for the armed response unit to arrive. Half an hour later, they spotted three of North Yorkshire's Volvo V70 vehicles pulling up and the team climbing out of them. SOCO were also due to arrive.

'He may know we're on to him,' said Turnbull. 'I think he'll head for the woodland which, unfortunately, will obscure him from our view. Maybe he'll head east to the A1 and try to hitch a lift north from a truck driver. Dave, call in and get a roadblock set up at Scotch Corner. Or maybe he'll head south, in which case we'd better get a roadblock set up at the junction of the A1 and A64.'

'I'm on to it,' said Jasper as he radioed HQ.

Turnbull knew the armed response unit would be equipped for every eventuality and that they would be trained in dynamic entry by the use of battering rams, if necessary. They would also have stun grenades, tear gas, crowbars, sledgehammers, tasers and pepper sprays and, of course, firearms for assailers and snipers.'

Turnbull could just see from above that they were clothed in fire-resistant material, boots and gloves with Kevlar helmets over a nomex balaclava. Each would have a secure radio, goggles, handcuffs and a first aid kit.

Turnbull spoke to the leader of the armed response unit by radio: 'Thanks for getting here so quickly. We've a triple murderer on the run and I thought it safer to ask for you boys. I'm in the chopper above you and I'll radio you if we get a sighting. We think he may have a gun. He certainly had, and may still have, a sheath knife which he's used to murder three people.'

'That's fine,' said the Inspector in charge of the armed response unit, a fit and highly-trained officer called Anthony Wardle. 'We'll track you from below.'

'George, let's get going,' said Turnbull. 'Head north first, about fifteen miles, then do a sweep using Masham as our centre point of the compass.'

'Okay, boss, no problem,' replied George as he turned the helicopter round and headed north. Turnbull and Jasper, whilst admiring the beautiful countryside below, kept their eyes open for a lone man. They flew over East Witton, where Turnbull recalled having taken Helen to the Blue Lion for lunch. Then they flew over Leyburn and south over moorland which had little cover. He kept the armed response unit aware of his route.

When they were near Lofthouse, Jasper shouted, 'Is that him? That man there running east.' Turnbull and George looked where Jasper was pointing and, true enough, a lone man was running across the moorland directly below them.

'Don't lose him, George,' said Turnbull. 'I'll report the sighting to Inspector Wardle. This isn't too far from where we last sighted them so they should get here pretty quickly.'

Having radioed in, they hovered for a while. 'Damn it,' said Turnbull. 'The bugger's gone to ground somewhere, he's not on the move, but we'll see him the minute he emerges. He must be in that old barn. It's the only conceivable hiding place for him with all that open countryside around.'

Within fifteen minutes, they spotted the three Volvos. Turnbull was again in radio contact with the Inspector Wardle.

'We think he's gone to ground in an old barn at OS grid reference SE102735. Can you form a circle round there and move in? Go carefully, he's dangerous.'

'Thanks, will do.'

Anthony Wardle had been in charge of the armed response unit for just over a year. He had joined the police force following his retirement from the SAS. He was a short man with black hair and was known in the force as being tough as old boots. He had been with the SAS for ten years, during which time he had done two fighting tours in Dhofar, Southern Oman, and he'd been in action in South Armagh, Northern Ireland.

He was pleased to have an active assignment. His men got bored protecting judges and courts when leaks had suggested that the defendants might be plucked or might try to escape. He had brought his men to the peak of fitness and was proud of them. His team comprised one photographer, five snipers and four assailers dressed in police combat fatigues. He would lead the assault team.

Wardle briefed his men: 'We believe that our suspect is holed up in that old barn you can just see four hundred yards to the east. We believe he may have a handgun, but we can't be sure. However, we do know that he's probably got a sheath knife which he's used to kill three people. There's a suggestion he's army trained but we don't know to what level. So, he's dangerous. We'll storm the barn and if he looks dangerous, go carefully. We don't want a manslaughter charge against us for shooting a suspect who hadn't a gun.'

Wardle deployed his men in different directions. The assailers, armed with 9mm carbines, encircled the barn and slowly closed in over open ground. The snipers' rifles, 7.62mm x 51mm scoped bolt-action, were trained on the barn door. Wardle went in with two of the assailers. He had a loud speaker with him. When he was about a hundred yards from the barn, he held position behind a solitary tree.

'This is the police. Come out. You are surrounded by an

armed response unit. If you emerge from the barn, come out of the door with your hands above your head and hold your knife in one hand and your gun, if you have one, in the other. We're closing in. If you attempt to resist, you may be shot by snipers whose rifles are trained on the barn.'

Slowly, the men encircling the barn closed in. There was no sign of the man surrendering. Wardle radioed Turnbull: 'Are you sure he's in there?'

'Ninety percent,' replied Turnbull. 'He can't be anywhere else. That's the point where he disappeared from our view.'

'Okay,' said Wardle. 'We'll go in.' He ordered two of the rifle officers to fetch the battering ram, which had been neatly strapped to the roof of one of the Volvos.

'Right, I want you two to lose that door,' ordered Wardle, pointing to a sturdy-looking wooden barn door.

The two men, wearing body-armour, ran at the door with the battering ram. The door shattered and fell inwards. Wardle and two others were close behind.

In the barn, there was no immediate sign of anyone. There were a few cows tethered in stalls on the one side. The whole floor was covered in straw, about nine inches thick and, of course, cow dung was liberally spread everywhere. By now, with the exception of one officer guarding the door, the entire team was in the barn.

'Right men,' said Wardle. 'He's in here somewhere. Look for pitchforks and start prodding. That'll flush him out.'

Two of the men found a couple of pitchforks leaning against the barn wall. They started at opposite ends of the barn, unoccupied by the cows, prodding the straw as they proceeded slowly towards each other. After a few prods, a man emerged covered in straw and cow dung and holding a knife in his right hand. The photographer immediately stepped forward and took a photo of him.

'All right, all right,' said the man. 'What's all the fuss about?'

'Drop the knife and move forward away from it so that it's out of your reach, then lie flat on the ground with your arms and legs outstretched.

'Okay, okay,' said the man as he proceeded to do as he was told.

Wardle approached him and told him he was being taken in for questioning.

'This is rubbish,' he said as he was being helped up, searched and handcuffed. He didn't have a gun.

Wardle radioed through to Turnbull who had watched the action from above.

'We've got him, sir. I've got your artist's impression and it's him alright. He's compliant. No trouble. He's cuffed and we're putting him in one of our vehicles. What do you want us to do with him?'

Turnbull had a lot of suggestions, but the one he communicated was: 'Take him to Bradford HQ, please, and thanks for your help. Great job.'

'Will do. Thanks, sir, that's what we're here for. We'll see you at HQ.'

Turnbull radioed the search party who, by now, were on Ilkley Moor: 'You can call off your search. We've got him. Many thanks.'

As George flew the helicopter southeast towards Leeds/ Bradford Airport, Turnbull radioed in to HQ to make sure they'd be ready and waiting for the man's arrival. As soon as they landed and had signed off the necessary paperwork, Turnbull and Jasper drove back to Bradford.

Meanwhile, the man was brought to Bradford. He was

checked into the custody suite by the custody sergeant and placed in a cell with two of the armed response team. He was told of his right to have someone informed of his arrest and to consult, privately, with a solicitor. He had made no comment.

Turnbull and Jasper arrived at Bradford HQ within an hour and went straight to the interview room. The man was brought in and told to sit down. He was handcuffed, extremely scruffy and smelly. Turnbull was struck by the likeness between the man's appearance and the artist's impression. He was wearing jeans and a zip-up jacket. The right leg of the jeans was blood-stained.

'Are you Arthur Mallinson?' asked Turnbull.

'Yes I am. What's this all about?'

'Arthur Mallinson, I am arresting you for the murders of Gordon Hodges, Amelia Hodges and David Hodges and for the rape of Amy Hodges on Friday the 26th of September 2008. You do not have to say anything, but if you fail to mention, when questioned, something you later reply on in court that may harm your defence. Anything you do say will be taken down and may be given in evidence.'

'I ain't committed no murders or rape,' replied Mallinson.

'You can go and have a shower, but your clothes will be retained for forensic examination. Do you understand?' said Turnbull whilst thinking how remarkably placid he was for a triple murderer.

'Yes, I understand,' Mallinson replied.

'You are entitled to a solicitor. Which solicitor would you like?'

'Richard Hodson from Hodson & Co in Bradford. He's helped me before.'

Really, thought Turnbull, *I thought he had no previous convictions.*

'I'll ring him and ask him to come here as soon as he can,' said Turnbull, thinking what a good case this will be for him and suspecting that Mallinson would be tried away from Bradford, which would make managing witnesses more difficult.

Turnbull noted that, when searched, Mallinson had no handcuffs with him yet he had retained the knife. *Odd,* he thought.

* * *

At 4:00 p.m., Richard Hodson arrived at Bradford HQ and was briefed by Turnbull about the allegations against his client. The solicitor conferred with Mallinson for one hour and then sent a message to Turnbull to say they were ready for the interview.

Turnbull and Jasper went to the largest interview room. Mallinson was brought in, handcuffed, and now accompanied by two prison officers, one on each side of him. Turnbull, at Hodson's request, agreed that the cuffs be removed. When that was done, Mallinson immediately relaxed.

'Now then, Arthur,' said Turnbull. 'My first duty is to caution you that you are not obliged to say anything, but if you fail to mention, when questioned, something you later reply on in court, that may harm your defence. Anything you do say may be given in evidence.'

Hodson interrupted to say he had advised his client about the caution.

Mallinson then said: 'I'm no murderer or rapist and I've never been to this house wherever it is.'

'When you were arrested, Arthur, did you have a knife with you?'

'Yes, I always carry one for my own protection. It's a sick world we live in these days. But I've murdered no one and I've not raped no one.'

'Well, Arthur, we suggest you somehow got into the house and murdered three people and raped a fourth.'

'Rubbish, I've never been to no house. I was on the run from Bingley Magistrates.'

'So, you never entered The Hollins at Middleton in Ilkley?'

'No.'

'You never had sexual intercourse with a girl there?'

'No.'

'Did you have handcuffs with you?'

'No.'

'Well, that'll do for the moment. When we have further material to hand, we'll interview you again on Monday. Is that convenient, Mr Hodson?'

'Yes,' replied Hodson who thought Mallinson had already disregarded his advice to say nothing. His denial of going to the house could come back to bite him.

With that, Mallinson was handcuffed and taken out by the two prison officers. Turnbull and Jasper went back to their office and Hodson returned to his.

At the end of another busy day, Turnbull and Jasper went to their respective homes.

The nights were now drawing in. Turnbull sat alone in his sitting-room, got out his pipe and poured himself a large Bell's whisky with ice and water.

What a Saturday, he thought. *It's not often one spies an escapee from a helicopter.* He'd enjoyed the beautiful views. He knew Mallinson had been stupid to deny presence at the house. His lies would count against him. *He's bound to change his story when the forensic evidence is disclosed to him,* he thought.

But, he wondered, *why carry handcuffs with him? And why didn't he wear gloves? He must have them for a reason. Did their possession mean he intended, in advance, to use them? If so, for what? To restrain a householder or a rape victim? Must make a note to check whether or not Talbot could tell if they were police issue. If so, he may have stolen them from that dopey lot at Keighley.* He made a note to ask Jane to check.

Turnbull sat and smoked his pipe and sipped his Scotch. *Helen must be out playing bridge,* he thought. He turned on the television and saw the artist's impression. 'Enough of that,' he said out loud as he switched off the television and put on some soothing music.

Chapter 7

On Monday, at 10:00 a.m., the group gathered in the conference room in the cell area. Professor Hughes, the odontologist, and Doctor Carr, the police surgeon, were also present together with Mr Hobson.

Turnbull cautioned Mallinson and said: 'We need to do some tests, Arthur. Are you willing to bite on this substance and to give us a sample of your blood and to be fingerprinted?'

'Yes, anything,' replied Mallinson. 'I'm innocent.'

'Well, that makes things easy. Thanks for your cooperation,' said Turnbull. 'This is Professor Hughes, he will supervise the bite.'

Professor Hughes produced a putty-like substance, similar to that used by dentists to get an impression of teeth. He said to Mallinson: 'This is polyvinyl siloxane. It has no taste and is totally harmless. Just bite on it, hold for a second and then release your bite.'

Mallinson did as he was requested and Professor Hughes removed the impression from his mouth.

'That's fine, no need for another,' said Hughes.

'Next, Arthur,' said Turnbull. 'Doctor Carr is a police surgeon and he's here to take a sample of your blood.'

'Needles frighten me,' said Mallinson as Doctor Carr proceeded to take a blood sample.

'Thank you, Arthur, that was very cooperative of you. And thank you gentlemen,' said Turnbull as Professor Hughes and Doctor Carr packed up their things and left the room.

'Now we need your fingerprints.' That was done by the Custody Sergeant who completed the task and then left the room.

'We'll leave you for a moment or two to relax, Arthur, with Mr Hobson. Would you like some tea?'

'Yes, please, milk and two sugars.

Turnbull couldn't believe how relaxed Mallinson was.

With that, the two policemen and Richard Hodson withdrew. Hodson thought to himself: *I'd advised him not to give those samples, but this guy thinks he knows best. Maybe he's forgotten he ate some cheese.*

* * *

The group reassembled at 11:00 a.m., by which time Turnbull had the results from two of the tests.

'Arthur, you're already under caution. I'd like to trace your movements from the time of your escape from the Magistrates' Court in Bingley. What can you tell me?'

'I've been on the run the whole time. I get claustrophobia and I had to get out of that stuffy room at court.'

'Did you go to Middleton in Ilkley?' asked Turnbull.

'No, I've already told you. Never been there in my life.'

'Well that's odd, Arthur, because we believe your blood is on the nightdress of a young woman called Amy Hodges, and your fingerprints are on a champagne bottle which was in the marquee at the house.'

'No way. There must be a mistake.'

'No mistake, Arthur. We believe it's your blood and your fingerprints. And I suspect, in time, we'll learn that it was your teeth that bit into the cheese that was in the refrigerator at the house.'

'I've never believed in science, me. You can stuff it as far as I'm concerned,' said Mallinson.

'So, where did you spend those days leading up to your arrest?' asked Turnbull.

'Living rough, like I told you,' said Mallinson. 'I got used to it when I was in the army. I like the open air and space. I get claustrophobia in enclosed places.'

'When were you in the army, Arthur?'

'When I was twenty. Only for a year, then they discharged me. Never knew why. That's when I had survival training.'

Bet I know why they discharged you, thought Turnbull, *because you're a mad man.*

'Well, Arthur, I am now charging you with the murders of Gordon Hodges, Amelia Hodges and David Hodges and with the rape of Amy Hodges. You do not have to say anything, but anything you do say will be taken down in writing and can be used during your trial.

'Yes. I have nothing else to say.'

With that, the meeting ended. Turnbull and Jasper went back to their room, Hobson to his office.

'You can get our men out of The Hollins and tell the marquee people they can take the marquee down,' said Turnbull. 'If she wishes, Amy can return to the house, although I very much doubt she'll want to. I can't help thinking about the poor lass. Can you find her GP and tell him or her what's happened and ask them to keep an eye on her?

'Just imagine not only losing your parents and brother, but being raped by their murderer.'

But at least the issue, so far, appears to be the identity of the murderer and rapist. God help the poor girl if the defence changes its mind when faced with the scientific evidence. Then she would have to be cross-examined about the rape and she won't like that, thought Turnbull.

Chapter 8

Turnbull's worries came true at the preliminary hearing at the Crown Court in Bradford where the case was due to be tried.

Counsel for the defence, Mr Mountfield, Q.C. and Mr Blackstone, who Turnbull knew had been in the *au pair trial* and the *honour killing trial*, looked glum.

The judge asked Mountfield if the defence had prepared a defence statement. They were obliged to provide one under the Police and Criminal Evidence Act, stating the defence and identifying those matters of evidence with which issue was taken.

'Yes, My Lord,' said counsel and handed the document in. A copy was handed to Turnbull. He was shocked at its contents, although he had expected something like this.

It read *"The defence admits that the defendant had sexual intercourse with Amy Hodges. The said intercourse was consensual and, therefore, rape is denied. The murders were committed by a person or persons unknown after the defendant had left the house."*

A good try, thought Turnbull, *but this line of defence didn't address the mother's blood being on Amy's nightdress, or the father's blood on her right foot, nor the handcuff marks on her wrists. Although, if Amy had tried to tend to her mother and father, that might explain the bloodstains.*

But what worried Turnbull was the prospect of Amy being cross-examined by counsel for the defence suggesting she consented to sex with Mallinson. If she was fragile now, she certainly would be after that. If the press were allowed to publish her identity, they would have a field day.

When the court adjourned, Turnbull went immediately to telephone Amy. Unsurprisingly, she was not at The Hollins so he telephoned her aunt's house where he found she was staying.

'I need to come and talk to Amy. Will it be convenient to you both if I come over at two o'clock this afternoon?'

'Yes, of course,' said her aunt. 'I'll make sure she's here. You've got my address, haven't you?'

'Yes, thank you, I will see you shortly,' replied Turnbull.

* * *+

Turnbull arrived at Amy's aunt's house, which was in Silsden, at 2:00 p.m. prompt. He was invited into the sitting-room where he found Amy looking much more composed than when he had last seen her, however, she looked pale and exhausted.

'I'll bring you some tea,' said Aunt Violet.

'Thank you, that would be nice,' said Turnbull as she left him alone with Amy. 'You're a strong young woman, Amy,' said Turnbull. 'Your mum, dad and brother would be very proud of you.'

'Thanks, but I haven't come to terms with it all yet. God knows what I'll be like when I do.'

'Amy, I have to tell you that there's been a new development in the case. Mallinson, who we believe committed the murders and raped you, has changed his defence. When confronted with the scientific evidence which proves his presence in the house, he's now saying that you agreed to have sex with him and that he left the house before your family was murdered.

'This, of course, does not get round the blood on your night-dress or on your right foot or, indeed, the handcuff marks. But we can't stop him raising this defence.'

Amy looked devastated.

'When faced with this,' continued Turnbull. 'We could not call you to give evidence at all and drop the rape charge, but that would leave the way clear for him to say, unchallenged, that you had consensual sex with him. No one would believe him, but that would be the effect. Or you can go ahead and give evidence.'

'No way am I going to let him do that,' said Amy, taking on board what Turnbull had told her. 'He raped me twice, the bastard. I owe it to my family to go into the witness box and nail him. He's evil and needs to be locked up for the rest of his life and if I can help to make sure that happens, I will give evidence.'

'Well, I hoped you'd say that, Amy,' said Turnbull. 'The defence will probably allege that you'd met him before. Is that a possibility?'

'What? That smelly, disgusting old man? No way.'

'How did he get into the house?' asked Turnbull.

'I've been thinking about that,' replied Amy. 'There's a patio door in the lounge which doesn't always engage properly. Dad had meant to get it fixed securely, but he and Mum had been so busy planning the wedding that they just never got round to it. It's easy to be wise after the event, isn't it?'

'So, his fingerprints will probably be on the patio door if that's where he gained entry,' said Turnbull. 'He wasn't wearing gloves.'

'If that's the way he got it, then yes,' said Amy.

'I'll get Bill Thornton to check that out,' said Turnbull. 'Now, Amy, I'm concerned for your welfare. We have a young lady detective in our squad. She's called Jane Rowley and you'll find her to be a very sympathetic and understanding woman and you can ring her at any time. I'll give you her card.'

'Thanks,' said Amy. 'That might help.'

Aunt Violet came into the room carrying a tray of tea and biscuits. *What a terrific lady,* thought Turnbull. *She's handling Amy so well and the results show.*

'How do you think Amy is doing?' Turnbull asked her.

'She has her ups and downs, but she's staying here as long as she wants. Aren't you, Amy?' said Violet as she set the tray down and poured out the tea. 'We're taking her away when it's convenient. Do we have to wait until after the trial?'

'If she were my niece, I'd take her away soon,' said Turnbull. 'And then I'd take her away again after the trial which will be at least three months away.'

'Good,' said Violet. 'When you've gone, we'll have a chat. I think some sunshine will do you good, Amy. I'll see if Jane and her husband can come as well.'

'I agree,' said Turnbull. 'I'm available any time, night or day, if you need me for anything at all.'

'Thank you. That's very reassuring and very kind of you,' said Violet.

'Has Amy seen her sister yet?' asked Turnbull.

'She's coming up tomorrow. Now she's married, she lives in London where George works. They cut short their honeymoon and only arrived back in London this morning. They'll drive up tomorrow morning.'

'That's good. By the way, Amy, have you thought of anything else since we last met?' asked Turnbull.

'I have actually. It was Aunt Violet who jogged my memory. When I was asked to identify Mum's body, it looked different. And then I remembered, her gold watch and her diamond necklace were missing. Were they recovered?'

'No,' said Turnbull. 'When we found her, she wasn't wearing either a watch or diamond necklace.'

'She was never without them,' said Amy.

'The watch was a present from Dad for their silver wedding anniversary. It was a Cartier,' said Amy.

'Was it photographed for insurance purposes?' enquired Turnbull.

'Yes, I imagine so. The photo will be in the household insurance file in the cabinet in Dad's study.'

'What about the necklace?' asked Turnbull.

'The same.'

'Would you mind coming back to the house with me to look?' asked Turnbull. 'Do you think you could handle that?'

'I think so, as long as Aunt Violet comes with us.'

'Don't worry, I will take you both there and bring you back. We don't have to stay long. I just need to see the photographs.'

Turnbull was very pleased with this news. *Mallinson had probably tried to fence the watch and necklace and that could be his mistake,* thought Turnbull.

Turnbull drove slowly and quietly to The Hollins. He rang Bill Thornton from the car to tell him about the patio door.

'I'll get over there ASAP and have a look at it,' said Bill. 'Can I get in?'

'Yes, we have a uniformed PC on duty at all times,' replied Turnbull.

They arrived at the gatehouse. Amy had a fob and was able to open the gates. They drove up the elegant drive.

'I know this is your first time back, Amy, so try to be strong,' said Turnbull.

The uniformed PC was on duty at the front door. He saluted Turnbull and opened the door. Turnbull, Aunt Violet and Amy went into the house and straight to her father's study.

Beneath a wooden work-surface, on which stood a computer, was a cupboard which Amy opened to reveal a grey filing cabinet. She pulled out the bottom drawer of the two-drawer cabinet which had *HOUSE* printed on a label on the front of it. She went to the *Household Insurance* file and pulled out the file entitled *Jewellery*. She opened it and there were several photographs of items of jewellery. Amongst them were the photographs of her mother's watch and necklace.

'Dad bought Mum the necklace in India,' explained Amy. 'Mum was always complaining that the diamonds came out of the clasps so Dad took it to Ogden's in Harrogate to have new clasps fitted. She also used to say the settings caught on her woollen garments but, nevertheless, she kept wearing it because she loved Dad so much.'

'Do you mind if I take the insurance documents and the photographs relating to the watch and necklace? I'll let you have them back,' asked Turnbull.

'No, of course not,' said Amy.

'Now we're here, can you say whether any other items were stolen?' asked Turnbull.

'No, I don't think so. Mum kept her other valuables in a safety deposit box at the bank.'

'Whilst we're here, do you mind walking round the exterior of the house with me?'

'No,' said Amy. 'I don't mind.'

They went outside. Turnbull always felt he'd missed something.

'Show me the insecure window you were telling me about, Amy.'

She led him round to the lounge window. Turnbull looked up above the window and there it was, a CCTV camera. *Bingo* he thought.

Turnbull wondered how he'd been so stupid. The first thing he should have looked for was a CCTV camera on a house of this size and importance. None of the team had suggested it either, which made him even more cross. *Well, what's done is done,* he thought, *time to move on.*

He tried to open the window from the outside. It was possible, just, but not without leaving fingerprints if you weren't wearing gloves.

'Amy, I need to recover the CCTV recordings from the time of the wedding on the 26th until midday on the 27th,' said Turnbull.

'No problem,' said Amy as they went back into the house and to her father's study. She switched on the computer. Turnbull was a bit of a philistine when it came to computers, so was happy to leave Amy to it.

'Will you be able to give me the recording I asked for?'

'Yes, but you'll have to ensure your computer is compatible with this tape,' said Amy.

'I'll call Jane,' said Turnbull. 'And ask her to come.'

Jane Rowley, the squad's computer expert, arrived forty minutes later, by which time Amy and Turnbull had looked at the recording several times. Turnbull was anxious that Amy didn't delete the recording by accident.

'Thanks for coming so quickly, Jane,' said Turnbull. 'Amy, this is DC Jane Rowley. She's the lady whose card I gave you.'

'Hello,' said Amy.

'Hello, Amy. I gather you're being a very brave girl. Don't forget, you can call me any time you want. Now, let me look at this recording,' said Jane.

They watched carefully and saw a man approaching the window at 10:12 p.m. The window opened, but Turnbull couldn't see if the man opened it or if it was opened from the inside. He couldn't see whether there was anyone inside. The window just reflected the light from the camera. The man had long, unkempt hair down to his shoulders and he was wearing what looked like a Parka and jeans, similar to what Arthur Mallison wore on arrest.

It certainly could be Mallinson as the clothing was consistent with it being his, but the quality of the recording was not good. Turnbull knew a lot of CCTV recordings were of similar poor quality. *If only people would invest in better equipment,* he thought, *it would give the police a far better chance of catching burglars.*

Jane's practised eye examined the recording carefully. Was the man wearing jewellery or spectacles? Was there any stain on the right leg of his jeans suggesting bleeding? How tall and thick set was the man? She would get the tape to Jeff Downs in the photographic department in the hope he could improve and enhance the image. Jane said she would go and that she'd let Turnbull know how she got on.

'Jane, whilst you're here, I want you to do something else for me, please,' said Turnbull. He produced the photographs of the watch and necklace. 'These are missing from Amy's mother's body. I want you to go to the usual jewellery fences we know to see if the thief tried to sell these items. It's expensive, a gold Cartier watch bought in the UK and a diamond necklace made in India. Worth a few grand I'd bet.

'Our man, when on the run, will have needed money quickly. He stole it between 10:00 p.m. and midnight on the 26th. He would try and fence it when the shops opened on the 27th. By that time, he could have travelled some distance. We know he headed north, so Skipton, Harrogate, Ripon, Masham are all possibilities. I suggest you cover those yourself.

'If he went east, before going north, then Knaresborough and York are both possibilities. If he went south first, then Shipley, Bradford and Leeds are possibilities. Get the details circulated and tell the other CID units to help you. You're in charge of identifying the fence and, hopefully, it was Mallinson who was trying to sell the jewellery. Once you've identified the fence, tell him we won't be prosecuting for handling stolen goods if they're helpful.'

'Will do,' said Jane. She took the CCTV recording and drove back to Bradford HQ where she gave the recording to Jeff Downs who relished the task of clarifying the recording and copying it for circulation.

Meanwhile, Bill Thornton went to examine the patio window.

Chapter 9

Jane got a list of well-known receivers from Sergeant Bob Hewitt in the Burglary Division. There would hardly be a receiver in West Yorkshire who Bob Hewitt didn't know. Of course, new ones emerged from time-to-time but, in the main, stolen jewellery went to established receivers, some of whom became police informers to avoid conviction.

'What's the stolen property?' he asked Jane.

'A gold Cartier watch and a diamond necklace worth several thousand pounds retail.'

'Well, he'll be lucky to get five hundred quid for both but I guess that would be enough for him to survive for a few weeks if he's on the run,' said Bob. 'You say you're covering west and northwest of Ilkley, so I'd try Fred Hardcastle in Skipton. Tread carefully with him. He's a good informant for our squad. He buys top end stuff.'

'Will do,' said Jane. 'I'll start in Ilkley and move northwest. I'll take young Jon Crawford with me. We'll pretend to be a couple.'

'Good ploy. Hitch your skirt up and wear something tight. They'll like that,' said Bob, thinking what shapely legs Jane had.

'You dirty bugger,' said Jane. 'But I'll follow your advice.'

Another sexist remark, she thought. She was used to them by now.

Two hours later, Jane and Jon, her new-found fiancé, had been to four jewellery and pawn shops in Ilkley and Keighley, without any luck. They made their way from Keighley to Skipton to pay Fred Hardcastle a visit. Her feet were killing her in her high heels and she was most uncomfortable in a tight, short skirt, which, as instructed, she had hitched up.

They arrived in Skipton and walked into Hardcastle's shop. A bell rang as they opened the door and a man emerged from the rear of the shop. Jane guessed he was in his fifties. He had a grey moustache and swept back hair in an effort, Jane thought, to look like Marlon Brando in *The Godfather*. She thought he was very creepy, especially when he ogled her from head to foot.

'Hello. Jon and I are looking for a nice gold watch. Nothing too expensive, but no questions asked, if you know what I mean. It's my birthday soon and Jon wants to buy me a watch, don't you darling?' said Jane.

'Yes,' said Jon meekly.

'Well, as it 'appens, I might just 'ave what you're looking for. It's just come in,' said Hardcastle in his broad Yorkshire accent. And, from under the counter, he produced a gold Cartier watch. 'It's a gem. Proper Cartier don't you know. None of that imitation rubbish. I'd say it's about twenty years old. It's yours for a grand.'

'I don't know,' said Jane. 'It's a bit more than we wanted to spend. Let me discuss this for a moment with my fiancé. Do you mind?'

'Not at all, take your time, love,' said Hardcastle.

Jane and Jon withdrew to the back of the shop where Jane produced a photograph of the stolen Cartier watch from her handbag. They compared the two and they were identical. It was more than likely to be the stolen watch or, if not, one identical to it.

Jane went back to Hardcastle who was standing, smiling, behind the counter. That is until Jane said: 'Bob Hewitt sends his regards.'

Jane produced her warrant card and said: 'I'm Detective Jane Rowley from the Bradford Homicide Squad and this is Detective Jonathan Crawford. I have a very good reason, Mr Hardcastle, for arresting you for handling stolen goods. You know that with your record, you'd get a minimum of three years. And when the court knows that this watch came from the house where a triple murder was committed, who knows what your sentence would be.

'But, on the other hand, you've been very helpful to Bob Hewitt in the past, so cooperation may allow us to be lenient with you. Who sold this to you?' asked Jane.

'Oh Christ,' said Hardcastle. He looked visibly shocked. 'Let me think for a moment.'

'Only a moment,' said Jane. 'And then you'll be under arrest.'

'Oh, all right. I only met him on Saturday. He said it was legit, honest. He said his mother had died and he needed the money to pay for the funeral.'

'And you believed him, did you? How much did you give for it?'

'Six hundred quid.'

'And what's it worth?'

'A few grand.'

'Have you been watching TV?' asked Crawford. 'Because a likeness of our killer has been plastered on the telly for the last forty-eight hours.'

'I don't watch telly, I'm too busy.'

'Did he give you a name?' asked Jane.

'No. Can I speak to Bob?' asked Hardcastle.

'Yes, okay, I'll get him for you,' said Jane as she got out her mobile and rang Bob's mobile number. 'Bob, it's Jane. I've got Fred Hardcastle with me and he wants to speak to you. I'll put him on.'

'Right,' replied Bob.

Hardcastle took Jane's phone and withdrew to the back of the shop. He spoke to Bob Hewitt and then returned to the counter. He said nothing.

'Finally, did he also sell you a diamond necklace made in India?' asked Jane.

'Yes, he did. It's here,' said Hardcastle as he produced it from under the counter.

'You are a naughty boy, Fred,' said Jane. 'Lucky you have a good friend in Bob Hewitt. You owe him one. Shut up shop. You're coming with us to Bradford to look at mug shots.

Hardcastle shut up his shop, leaving a *CLOSED* sign on the door. He turned on his alarm. 'Can't be too careful these days,' he said.

What a hypocrite thought Jane as they got in the car.

The three travelled to Bradford where Jane left Hardcastle with Jonathan Crawford.

Jane then went to see how Jeff Downs had got on with the CCTV recording. It was much clearer than it had been on the Hodges' computer. She examined it frame-by-frame, hoping to see some feature which identified the man. However, there was nothing she could see which helped.

Next, she returned to Hardcastle and Jonathan who were having a coffee in the canteen. 'Come with me, 'she said and took Fred Hardcastle to look at the recording. He did so, but couldn't say whether the man shown was the one who sold him the watch and necklace. *You win some, you lose some,* thought Jane.

Jane then organised a viper identification parade. This involved twelve mug-shots of people of similar build, etc. to Mallinson and included one of Mallinson himself at number five. It was conducted by officers independent of the enquiry, as required by the Police Criminal Evidence Act. Hardcastle was asked if he could pick out the man who sold him the jewellery.

'Yes, it's number five. I'm pretty sure it's number five,' he said.

'What about his voice?' asked the officer in charge.

'I'd say Geordie. He was very dirty and dishevelled.'

Jane was told what had happened by the officer in charge of the parade.

'Thank you for your help, Mr Hardcastle,' said Jane. 'I'll get someone to drive you back to Skipton.'

Bingo, thought Jane, *we now have an identification of Mallinson by the purchaser of the stolen jewellery.*

Chapter 10

Turnbull drove straight home after seeing Amy. He felt upset. The job didn't often get to him, but this time, for some reason, it had. He thought it must be because he was seeing this young girl being so brave. When he got home, Helen, his wife, was there. He was so pleased to see her.

'You're home early,' she said as she greeted him with a kiss. 'You look a bit down. Is something the matter?'

'This murder and rape case I'm handling, it's really getting to me. This poor girl, who was left alive, is now alone, apart from her sister who's just got married and is living in London. I can't imagine what turmoil she's in, but she's being so brave. She's staying with her aunt and uncle at the moment.'

'Never mind, love,' said Helen. 'Go and sit in the garden and put your feet up whilst I make you a nice cup of tea.'

Turnbull made his way out on to the terrace. He was thinking about his team and wondering if it was affecting them like it was affecting him. If, at his age, he was touched by this one, surely it must have affected the others. Yet, Dave Jasper showed no signs of being upset by it all. *He's a cool customer, our Dave,* he thought, *but maybe a bit too cool. As for Jane, maybe it will affect her.* Jon Crawford was with Jane. He was a young detective who'd come back from the Leeds Vice Squad, with which he's spent a few months. Turnbull could do with that extra pair of hands.

Turnbull was thinking about the case: *Why oh why did Mallinson have handcuffs? He obviously intended, if necessary, to handcuff someone. And where did he get them?*

Meanwhile, Bill Thornton was back at The Hollins testing

for fingerprints on the patio door. There were none on the outside, but plenty on the inside which were not Mallinson's. *Hmm,* he thought to himself, *if he wasn't wearing gloves, surely we would have found some prints even if smudged on the patio window? Could he have been let in?*

Chapter 11

Turnbull was in his office early the following day, catching up on paperwork relating to some non-urgent cases which had been neglected because of the Mallinson case. The telephone rang. It was Dave Jasper.

'Sir, we've just had a confession to the Hodges' murders from a man called Patterson who lives in Ilkley. I think he's a nutcase, but I don't suppose we can ignore it. We'd have to disclose it to the defence anyway, whether or not it's nonsense, so we'd better take it seriously.'

Turnbull knew he was right. If the police found any material which may be of assistance to the defence, there was a duty on the police to disclose it to the defence. If they were discovered not doing so, it could lead to a conviction being overturned by the Court of Appeal.

'I agree,' said Turnbull. 'Arrest him and bring him in. That'll make him sit up. We'll interview him at noon.'

'Will do,' said Jasper.

Oh, hell, thought Turnbull, *this will make what we thought was a straightforward case messier.*

He remembered this happening years ago in a murder case when, unusually, prosecution counsel called the evidence of a nutcase's confession as part of the prosecution case in order to discredit it before the defence got hold of it. The judge could not understand the prosecution tactics and said so, but he didn't interfere.

What's the betting, thought Turnbull, *that this Patterson chap hasn't a clue what happened.* Unfortunately, the press had published quite a few details, so if he'd read some of the press coverage, he'd have a good idea what had happened. Fortunately, the police hadn't disclosed the rape allegation, or the location of the bodies, or the dimensions of the knife used in the murders, or the method of entry into the house, *So, we'll see what, if anything,* thought Turnbull, *he says about those things.*

At noon, Patterson was brought in by Jasper and they met Turnbull in the interview room. Patterson was about the same age as Mallinson with similar long, unruly hair. He was about the same height and build. He had several convictions for house burglary in the Menston and Otley area. *Fairly close by,* thought Turnbull, as he turned on the tape recorder.

'Do you want a solicitor, Mr Patterson?' asked Turnbull.

'No thanks,' Patterson replied.

'First, Mr Patterson, it's my duty to caution you,' said Turnbull, which he proceeded to do in the usual terms.

'Now then,' said Turnbull. 'I understand you want to make a confession. Of what, may I ask?'

'Of those three murders of the Hodges family.'

'Anything else?'

'No, that's enough isn't it? I've had a grudge against that man Hodges ever since he sacked me. I was a wool sorter at one of his mills. In Halifax it was. Out of the blue, for no reason, he gave me a DCM.'

'What's a DCM?' asked Jasper.

'A *Don't Come Monday.* He sacked me on the spot on the Friday and that was it. I've never managed to get a job after that. The bastard. I've been unemployed the last ten years.'

Not surprised, thought Turnbull.

'Did you read about these murders in the newspaper?' asked Turnbull.

'It was in the *Yorkshire Evening Post,* but I knew all about it, cos I did it.'

'How many people were in the house?'

'Just them three. Mr and Mrs and their son.'

'Why kill Mrs Hodges and their son?'

'Why not? I'll get life for one so I thought I might as well kill all three. It serves 'em right.'

'How did you kill them?'

'I stabbed them.'

'Where?'

'In the heart.'

'What, all three?'

'Yes, I stabbed all three in the heart. They deserved it.'

'What did you do when you were in the house? Did you drink or eat anything?'

'No.'

'How did you get in?'

'I broke in, didn't I? I smashed in the front door. They were all out. They came back when I was looking for things to steal.'

'And where were they when you stabbed them?'

'I can't honestly remember.'

'Why not? Just picture the event in your mind and tell me where they were.'

'I think they were all in the sitting room discussing the break in and having a drink.'

'So, they came home to find the front door smashed in and calmly went into the sitting room to have a drink?'

'Yes, probably to calm there nerves.'

'Did anyone resist?'

'Yes, the boy tried to stop me, but I stabbed him first and then the other two.'

'So, they were all dead in the sitting room?'

'Yes.'

'What sort of knife did you use?'

'A carving knife I took from home.'

'Where is it now?'

'In my kitchen drawer.'

'You'll be able to give it to us then?'

'No problem. I've washed it though, so you won't find any blood on it.'

'What had been happening that day?'

'Like it said in the papers, they'd had a wedding in a big tent in the garden.'

'Did you ever go in the marquee?'

'No, why should I?'

'Did you enter and manage to steal anything?'

'No, they came back before I had a chance.'

'Well, thank you, Mr Patterson. DS Jasper will take you home and you can give him your carving knife. You are, for the moment, free to go.'

'What? Aren't you going to lock me up?'

'Not at the moment, no. Have you ever confessed to murder before?'

'No, of course not. These are the first murders I've done.'

'Have you ever before confessed to a crime you did not commit?'

'No, what do you think I am? A nutcase?'

I'm not answering that, thought Turnbull, but his experience of false confessions was that they waste a huge amount of police time. *I can do without this,* he thought as he left the interview room. He would have the interview transcribed and disclosed to the defence team who would make of it what they will.

When he returned to his office, Turnbull rang Professor Talbot: 'Sorry to trouble you, Prof, but I need some more info in a supplemental report. Is it possible that the wounds to Mr and Mrs Hodges and their son were caused by a carving knife?'

'I would say that the wound to the throat of David Hodges could have been, but not the stab wounds to Mr and Mrs Hodges. The knife used on those two victims was a Bowie or sheath knife with a four-inch-wide, one-sided blade. Have you got this carving knife?'

'Not yet, but I'll have it shortly.'

'Well, let me see it, but I doubt very much that a carving knife was used in this case.'

'As soon as we have the knife, I'll ask DS Jasper to deliver it to you. How long before you'll be able to let me have the supplemental report?'

'A few days at the most. I'll have it e-mailed to you.'

'Thanks, Prof.'

Dave Jasper returned with the knife which he duly took to Prof Talbot's laboratory. True to his word, two days later, Prof Talbot's supplemental report arrived by e-mail. It read: *As I said on the telephone, the wounds to Mr Gordon Hodges and Mrs Amelia Hodges were not caused by this carving knife, although that to David could have been.*

Turnbull e-mailed his thanks to the Professor and then he sent the transcript of the interview with Patterson, the supplemental report and the carving knife over to Myles Gibson at the CPS. Forensics confirmed that there was no blood on the knife.

Chapter 12

James Turnbull was in his office thinking that the killer and rapist was now in custody. Although, on the face of it, Mallinson was denying being the killer, Turnbull thought him banged to rights. He was in the house, established by his fingerprints on the champagne bottle and his bite marks in the cheese. The mother and father's blood on Amy's nightgown established a nexus between the rape and the murders and the handcuff marks on Amy's wrists corroborated her version that he raped her.

This trial would be straightforward. With a bit of luck, Hardcastle would identify Mallinson and he had a good team to prosecute in Beecroft and Oldroyd. His part in the whole judicial process was all but over. He might be needed for the odd enquiry during the trial. Would there, however, be a hitch? In Turnbull's experience whenever things seemed to be going swimmingly, there was a hitch.

At that very moment, his telephone rang. *Is this the hitch?* he wondered.

'Sir, Desk Sergeant here. I have a gentleman here who is anxious to see you. He's a captain. He says it's to do with the Mallinson case. He says he's got some very important and relevant information. He's undoubtedly authentic. He showed me his card. He's from the Security Services. I thought you would want to see him.'

'Thanks, Sergeant, bring him up,' said Turnbull thinking that his hitch was now manifesting itself.

A few minutes later, there was a knock on his door. 'Come in,' said Turnbull.

The sergeant entered the room first, followed by a very smart-looking army officer: 'This is Captain Clarke, sir,' said the sergeant as he then took his leave. Captain Clarke reminded Turnbull of Andrew Strauss, the young cricketer. Turnbull introduced himself as he shook his hand and invited him to take a seat.

'I gather you have Arthur Mallinson in custody and that he's been charged with the triple murder of the Hodges family and with the rape of their daughter,' said Captain Clarke.

Turnbull thought he spoke of it as though it was a motoring offence.

'That's true,' said Turnbull. 'We definitely believe we have the right man.'

'I don't doubt it,' said the captain. 'But do you know who he is?'

'I have no doubt that you're going to tell me.'

'Well, in normal circumstances, if there was nothing of great moment facing him, I would be able to exert considerable pressure on you to drop the charges. But I recognise that, in this instance, Arthur has gone too far to only receive a rap on the knuckles.'

'You're talking in riddles,' said Turnbull. 'Please get to the point.'

'Please be patient, Detective Chief Inspector,' said Captain Clarke. 'What I am about to tell you is highly confidential and is not, without my permission, to go beyond these four walls.'

'By what authority to you say that to me?' asked Turnbull.

'Will your Home Secretary do? He is, after all, in your overall command, is he not?' said Captain Clarke as he produced his card and handed it across the desk to Turnbull.

Turnbull looked at the card which said *Captain Michael Clarke, Thames House,* followed by a telephone number.

Turnbull knew Thames House to be the MI5 headquarters.

'That telephone number is fictitious,' said Captain Clarke. 'But if you wish to check my credentials, please ring this number.' He handed him a piece of paper bearing nothing but a telephone number.

I'm not taking anything this man says at face value, thought Turnbull, as he rang the number.

'Please may I have that piece of paper back?' asked Captain Clarke. Turnbull pushed the slip of paper to him across the desk as he waited for the call to be answered.

'Home Office,' was the response. 'Which extension number do you require?'

'Extension number?' said Turnbull.

Clarke intervened: 'Tell her 222.'

'222,' said Turnbull to the lady at the Home Office.

'What security clearance do you have?' she asked.

'Security clearance?' repeated Turnbull.

'Just say you have Captain Michael Clarke with you and I'll speak to her.'

'I have Captain Michael Clarke with me,' repeated Turnbull. 'I will put him on the phone.'

'Clarke here, I am with DCI Turnbull and he wants clearance to speak to me.' He handed the phone to Turnbull. 'Please tell her this number, sixty-five.'

'DCI Turnbull, here, sixty-five.'

'That's Captain Clarke all right,' she said. 'You can take it that he is acting with the full authority of the Home Secretary.'

'Thank you for your help,' said Turnbull as he replaced the receiver.

'How do I know the number you gave me is the Home Office?' asked Turnbull.

'Do whatever check you want,' replied Clarke.

Turnbull rang the switchboard and asked them to ring the Home Office.

The sergeant rang back: 'It's the Home Office alright.'

Turnbull turned his attention to Clarke: 'And in what way can I assist you, Captain Clarke.'

'It's more a case of how can I assist you?' said Clarke. 'Mallinson is a secret asset, a mole if you like, for HM Government, within the IRA. You may have wondered how such a violent man has a non-existent record of offending. You may also have wondered why you have no photograph of him or his fingerprints on police files. That is our doing.

'Arthur's history is very interesting. His uncle is from Belfast. Arthur lived with him for two years. He was, at an early age, indoctrinated into the IRA. After that, he was caught in a roadblock which had been put in place after Earl Mountbatten's assassination in southern Ireland in 1979. He was, by then, a fully-fledged member of the IRA and on the face of it remained as such. We, however, turned him so that since then he has been our secret asset within the IRA; a mole within and a very valuable one too.

'He has many qualities, our Arthur Mallinson. He is skilled in surveillance, armed combat and survival techniques. We trained him thoroughly. He is a psychopath with no compunction about killing. He's been responsible for a number of undetected sectarian killings of prominent members of the IRA, which remain unsolved. He's been an invaluable source of information of IRA plots. You may remember Roy Mason was Secretary of State for Northern Ireland in the Wilson government in the late seventies. Arthur's information prevented his assassination. His information has foiled several plots. He is ruthless and very much trusted by the IRA and by us.

'He's getting older now, is our Arthur, but you'd never have found him without a helicopter. I bet you wondered how he escaped from the Magistrates' Court. He can wriggle through virtually any hole. He's highly skilled, is our Arthur.'

'This is all very interesting,' said Turnbull, 'but what can I do for you? He has committed an appalling triple murder and a rape.'

'Well, we realise this is too serious for us to bring pressure on you to let him off, as we have done in the past,' said Clarke. 'But we would like, what is known in our trade, as a *White Envelope* to be passed to the judge. This is a well-recognised method of passing secret information to a judge which is never openly referred to in court.'

Turnbull knew of this, but had never before been involved with a *White Envelope.*

'He's a lady's man, is our Arthur. I bet you found no sign of a forced entry,' said Clarke.

That's true, thought Turnbull.

'What evidence have you against him?' asked Clarke.

Turnbull explained.

'But the girl could have walked through the blood and gone to her mother after the so-called rape,' said Clarke.

'That's true,' said Turnbull. 'But not according to the rape victim and she is rock solid. How could he explain the handcuff marks?'

'I accept that Arthur's a loose cannon,' said Clarke. 'He has obviously gone off the rails this time. What was he in custody for?'

'Nothing much,' replied Turnbull. 'A house burglary.'

'Quite why he committed these murders and this rape, I can't tell you,' said Clarke. 'He's normally well-controlled. He must have gone off the rails for some reason. We will miss him. He's a very useful asset and I want the judge to reflect that in a lesser sentence. He's been working for HM Government in a positive way for years and we want to make sure the sentencing judge knows that.'

'But, if I understand you correctly,' said Turnbull, 'he was involved in the beginning in the assassination of Earl Mountbatten.'

'That's true, along with others, but he's made amends since,' said Clarke.

'I don't think Prince Charles would agree with you,' said Turnbull thinking of the deep affection in which Prince Charles held his uncle.

'Well, that's all water under the bridge,' said Clarke. 'In the event of conviction, I will deliver to you a *White Envelope* which you must ensure is delivered to the judge.'

'What, without our counsel knowing?'

'The fewer who know, the better,' said Clarke.

'How do I get in touch with you?' asked Turnbull.

'You don't. After this meeting, no one will acknowledge my existence,' said Clarke. 'Oh, by the way, I feel I owe Arthur some allegiance for all he has done. Is there anything which might help him?'

'Well, we had the usual nutcase ringing up and confessing,' said Turnbull. He didn't think there was any harm disclosing this to Clarke as it had to be disclosed to the defence in any event.

'Oh, who was that?' asked Clarke.

'A man called Patterson. We interviewed him. He didn't know the basic facts and we dismissed him as a crank.'

'Oh, really,' said Clarke as he stood up and extended his arm across the desk to shake Turnbull's hand. 'Nice meeting you. If I want to be in touch, I know where to find you, although not the other way around.'

'Yes, nice meeting you,' said Turnbull as Clarke turned and left his office. *Well, there's more to our Arthur Mallinson than meets the eye,* thought Turnbull, *and a shame that no finger-prints of Mallinson had been found on the outside of the patio door. Oh well, you can't have everything.*

Chapter 13

The next few weeks were spent getting ready for the trial. Turnbull always found this the most boring part of his job. He met Myles Gibson from the CPS and gave him the witness statements his team had garnered during their investigations. The CPS would decide what to serve as the prosecution case and what to disclose to the defence as material not to be used in the prosecution case.

The Weatherheads, the uniformed police first at the scene, himself and Jasper, Bill Thornton and his SOCO team, the police surgeon and the pathologist, Fred Hardcastle, Jane Rowley and, of course, Amy, were the witnesses Turnbull expected to be called for the prosecution.

Amy's evidence was crucial as to the identity of the killer and the rape of herself. Turnbull knew that, for the rape, he needed corroboration. The distress wasn't enough as it was equally consistent with her reaction to the murder of her family. Turnbull also knew that the handcuff marks were absolutely crucial and the pathologist's, John Talbot, evidence as to their cause was capable of corroborating her allegation of rape.

The evidence as to the knife used in the murders being identical to the one Mallinson was in possession of, when arrested, was also crucial.

The fact that Amy had no damage to her private parts didn't help, but he knew that submission wasn't the same as consent. If her story was to be believed, she just let him do it when petrified that he would kill her as he had done her brother and her parents.

Turnbull remembered to ring DCI Lythe at Keighley police

station: 'Turnbull here,' he said without pleasantries. 'Can you tell me whether any handcuffs went missing when you had Mallinson in custody?'

'Not so far as I am aware. I'll check with the Custody Officers. Hold on.'

Turnbull waited a couple of minutes before Lythe came back on the phone: 'We don't have an inventory of handcuffs, so we can't say whether any are missing.'

'Did Mallinson have access to them at any time?' asked Turnbull.

'Only when he was with the Custody Sergeant. There may have been a pair on his desk. It was very busy,' replied Lythe.

God, thought Turnbull, *this nick is outrageous.*

'Thanks,' said Turnbull and rang off.

Turnbull said to Jasper: 'We've got a consultation with counsel at two o'clock in Park Square, Leeds.' Myles Gibson had chosen Beecroft and Oldroyd to prosecute. They were favourites with the CPS. 'Fancy some lunch first?'

'Okay,' said Jasper. 'Can we go for a curry to the Aagrah, it's on our way to Leeds?'

'Fine by me,' said Turnbull as they headed for the well-known Indian restaurant in Bradford.

* * *

Consultation with counsel was much as usual. Turnbull, Jasper and Myles Gibson were ushered into the Silk's (QC's) conference room. Coffee and biscuits were on hand. Beecroft and Oldroyd entered the room. Both, as usual, looked immaculate. Beecroft with his old school bow tie and Oldroyd in his black jacket and striped trousers.

'Well, thank you for briefing us,' said Beecroft. 'As usual, the case has been well prepared. Amy Hodges is at the centre of the whole case. How's she standing up?' he asked Turnbull.

'Well, except that she wasn't best pleased when she heard of his change in defence, nor will she be if the court allows her identity to be disclosed. She's being taken abroad by her aunt and uncle for a break. I understand the trial date is Wednesday, 10th of December, before Mr Justice Griffiths,' said Turnbull.

'Your report about MI5's involvement is a bit strange,' said Beecroft. 'And the fact that they've managed to keep him out of trouble is even stranger. MI5 will probably put their oar in before the end of the case. Watch this space. Don't disclose to the defence what you know about them. Apparently, you were told not to tell me, but I'm grateful you did.'

'Is there anything you want us to do?' asked Turnbull, not having mentioned the *White Envelope*.

'This man, Patterson, who came in and confessed,' said Beecroft. 'Check out his history. Find out if he's made false confessions before. Normally such confessors have a history of this behaviour. They like to be in the public eye and know that they'll never be prosecuted because what they are saying doesn't fit with the known facts. I wouldn't be surprised if the defence don't try and make something of his confessions. They may even call him as a witness for the defence, so make enquiries about him.'

'The important thing,' said Turnbull. 'Is that we've got Mallinson in the house. The chances of a mystery man arriving after him and committing the murders are very remote.'

The group went on to discuss witnesses and dates when the witnesses should be at court to give evidence. The meeting adjourned at 4:00 p.m.

Chapter 14

The trial was set down for hearing before Mr Justice Griffiths. Turnbull knew the judge well from previous cases he had tried. His career was as a Treasury Counsel when he prosecuted at the Old Bailey (Central Criminal Court) before becoming a permanent judge at the Old Bailey and, finally, a High Court Judge. The Lord Chancellor's department used him almost exclusively for high profile murder trials all over the country, such as this one.

Despite his background as a prosecutor, Turnbull always found him to be fair and he had the great skill of seldom interrupting and asking questions. This was a failing of many judges who seemed to forget they were no longer prosecuting at the Bar. Griffiths, in contrast, was quiet and courteous to all in his court and that was a great asset.

Turnbull remembered, when he was a Detective Sergeant, arresting a Dutchman who was tried for importing a huge quantity of cocaine. The Circuit Judge, trying the case, kept interrupting and making pro-prosecution remarks. He was sarcastic and difficult with the defence. Prosecuting counsel always hate judges doing this because jurors interpret such behaviour as unfair to an accused.

After numerous such interruptions, in one of which he referred to very senior defence counsel's question as "facile", prosecuting counsel stood and said he wished to say something in the absence of the jury.

'Oh, very well,' said the judge impatiently. The jury left court and the judge said: 'Yes, what is it?'

Prosecuting counsel said: 'If Your Honour persists in

making such prejudicial remarks, the Crown will concede at the Court of Appeal that the accused did not have a fair trial.'

This shut the judge up and he didn't say a dicky bird thereafter because he knew that with such a concession by the prosecution, an appeal against conviction may well succeed on the ground that the accused did not have a fair trial.

The court staff also liked Griffiths. He enjoyed coming to try cases on the North-Eastern Circuit as it was rumoured he had relatives who lived in Pateley Bridge.

The judges always stayed at Carr Manor, the Judges' Lodgings in Leeds. Griffiths was known to enjoy a night out at the Grand Theatre listening to Opera North.

Turnbull remembered the days when the High Court Judge sitting in Leeds would arrive at court from Carr Manor in a judicial Rolls Royce with outriders. He would go back to Carr Manor in the same style for lunch and would often ask counsel from both sides who were appearing in front of him, to have lunch with him. Those days had long gone. The judges now had a sandwich in their room and came to court without outriders.

Turnbull remembered a story about one notoriously difficult High Court Judge being given a V sign by a member of the public as he passed in his Rolls with outriders. The judge had him hauled before him for contempt of court. The poor man's explanation for his behaviour was that he thought the judge was the Lord Mayor whom he thought was, as he put it, *"a right pillock"*. He said he was very sorry and no offence to the judge was intended. He was let off with a warning to be careful who he gave V signs to in future.

* * *

The court was already full by 10:00 a.m. on the first day of the trial. Turnbull and Jasper sat behind Myles Gibson, the CPS representative. He sat behind junior counsel for the prosecution who in turn sat behind Mr Beecroft, Q.C., leading counsel for the Crown. The defence team sat in the same order further down counsels' bench.

The gallery became full and the ushers were having to turn people away. The press gallery was also full. Turnbull recognised a few pressmen and women. The others, he assumed, were from the Nationals and television. This trial would be of great national interest as it involved three murders of one prominent Yorkshire family. Turnbull didn't know how the press would handle the rape as, at present, they were not permitted to report anything which would lead to the identification of Amy, as the victim of rape, without the leave of the judge. However, Turnbull spied an extra Q.C. and it soon became apparent why he was in court.

'All rise,' said the clerk at precisely 10:30 a.m. The judge came into court in his red robes with an ermine sash. He wore his Court Judge's wig. He bowed to counsel who bowed back.

The case was called on. Mallinson came from the cells escorted, in handcuffs, by two prison officers.

Beecroft stood to address the judge: 'My Lord, there are three preliminary matters upon which counsel require a ruling before the trial begins. Your Lordship knows the representation, but may I introduce my learned friend Mr Barnet who represents the Press Association. He wishes to address you now but, before he does, would your Lordship make an order under the Contempt of Court Act that nothing which Mr Barnet is about to say can be reported, nor any response thereto.'

'I make such an order,' said the judge.

'Yes, My Lord,' said Mr Barnet as he stood. 'I represent the

Press Association which is placed in an impossible position when it comes to reporting this trial which has huge public interest. A major witness for the Crown is Amy Hodges who not only speaks to the murders, but who also speaks to her own rape. The evidence she gives is of one continuous event. The law, as you know, forbids reporting a rape if it will lead to the identification of the rape victim. This is, as you know, under the Sexual Offences (Amended) Act 1992, Section 1(1).

'It will be impossible for the press to report this trial in a meaningful way without such a report leading to the identification of Amy Hodges as the victim of the rape.

'If the press tries to report it, leaving out any reference to her rape, it will distort the effect of her testimony. Therefore, reluctantly, we are left in a position of having to ask your Lordship to allow Amy Hodges' name to be published in connection with both the murders and the rape.

'We submit, under Section 3(2) of the Act that you have a discretion to allow her name to be published if you are satisfied that the effect of Section 1 is to impose a substantial and unreasonable restriction upon the reporting of these proceedings and that it is in the public interest to remove or relax the restriction. We submit you should be so satisfied. That, My Lord, is my submission.'

'Thank you, Mr Barnet. Do the prosecution have any observations?' asked the judge.

'No, My Lord,' said Beecroft. 'The Crown is neutral on this issue.'

'Nor I, My Lord,' said Mountfield. 'The defence is also neutral.'

'Thank you, gentlemen. My ruling is that restriction will be removed. The press may report the proceedings in full, including the name of the rape victim.'

God, thought Turnbull, *not only is Amy going to be put through the hoop of cross-examination, but her name as the victim of rape is going to be plastered all over the country's press.* Turnbull decided to tell Amy about the judge's ruling. He whispered to Jasper, 'Go and tell Amy her name is to be published.'

Jasper went out of court to speak to Amy who was in the witness room. He told her the news which she accepted. She could understand why and had expected something like this.

Meanwhile, in court, Beecroft stood again: 'Next, My Lord, the prison officers require a ruling as to whether or not Mallinson should be handcuffed during his trial.'

'The defendant escaped from lawful custody, did he not?' asked the judge.

'Yes, My Lord, when at Bingley Magistrates' Court and under guard by G4S, not the prison service,' said Beecroft.

'What do you say, Mr Mountfield?' asked the judge.

Mountfield stood and said: 'Mallinson will, in all probability, be giving evidence in this trial. His credibility may be affected adversely if, during his evidence, he is handcuffed.'

'I agree,' said the judge. 'I order that he be handcuffed except when in the witness box. And when in the dock, I ask that handcuffing be as discreet as possible.'

'Thank you, My Lord,' said counsel in turn.

Beecroft stood. 'My Lord, finally I ask permission for Detective Chief Inspector Turnbull and Detective Sergeant Jasper to be in court throughout the trial. They are heavily involved in this investigation as the officers in this case. I am told by my learned friend that there is to be no dispute as to their evidence.'

'Any objection, Mr Mountfield?' asked the judge.

'No, My Lord.'

'So be it,' said the judge. 'They may be present throughout the trial.'

That's excellent, thought Turnbull, *we can follow things as they occur.*

The jury panel then came into court and stood at the back of the court.

The judge addressed counsel: 'Will this case finish in the two weeks for which jurors have been asked to serve as jurors?'

'Yes, My Lord,' said counsel in turn.

'Very well, let the jury be sworn,' said the judge.

The court clerk stood and directed her comments to Mallinson who stood in the dock with a burly prison officer on either side of him. His handcuffs could not be seen by those not in the dock.

'Arthur Mallinson,' she said. 'You are indicted with the offences of murder and rape. By the first count, you are charged with murder and the particulars are that on the twenty-sixth day of September 2008, you murdered Gordon Hodges. How do you plead, guilty or not guilty?'

'Not guilty, My Lord.'

'By the second count, you are charged with murder and the particulars are that on the twenty-sixth day of September 2008, you murdered Amelia Hodges. How do you plead, guilty or not guilty?'

'Not guilty, My Lord.'

'By the third count, you are charged with murder and the particulars are that on the twenty-sixth day of September 2008, you murdered David Hodges. How do you plead, guilty or not guilty?'

'Not guilty, My Lord.'

'By the fourth count, you are charged with rape and the particulars are that on the twenty-sixth day of September 2008, you raped Amy Hodges. How do you plead, guilty or not guilty?'

'Not guilty, My Lord.'

'Arthur Mallinson, the names I am about to call are the names of the jurors who will try you. If you object to them, or to any of them, the time to do so is as they come to the book to be sworn and before they are sworn and your objection will be heard.'

The clerk then called out the names of the twelve jurors who took their place in the jury box. Each of them then took an oath on the Testament saying "I swear by Almighty God that I will faithfully try the defendant and give true verdicts according to the evidence".

The jurors not called were released and sent to the Jury Waiting Room to be available for other trials. Turnbull noted to himself, *no objections to any juror.*

The jurors were a mixed bag of varying ages, six women and six men, all white. One man carried the *Times* newspaper. *He'll probably be the Foreman,* thought Turnbull. They looked understandably apprehensive as no doubt they had seen or read about these murders on the television and in the papers but not, so far, the rape. Some would enjoy the experience of being a member of the jury, others would hate it. The decision they were about to make would either condemn Mallinson to a life in prison or set him free into the public, maybe with doubts as to his dangerousness.

'Members of the jury, are you all sworn?' asked the clerk. She continued: 'The defendant, Arthur Mallinson, stands indicted for that he on the 26th of September 2008, murdered Gordon Hodges, Amelia Hodges and David Hodges and raped Amy Hodges. To this indictment he has pleaded not guilty and it is your duty to say, having first heard the evidence, whether he is guilty or not of any or all of the charges.'

The judge then turned to the jury and said: 'You will now hear an opening speech from leading counsel for the Crown outlining the Crown's case.'

Beecroft stood and said: 'May it please your Lordship, members of the jury, I appear together with my learned friend Mr Oldroyd, who sits behind me, for the Crown. The defendant, Arthur Mallinson, is represented by my learned friends Mr Mountfield and Mr Blackstone.'

Defence counsel nodded to the jury, identifying themselves.

Mr Beecroft continued: 'Members of the jury, the 26th September 2008 started as a day of supreme happiness for the Hodges family. The elder daughter, Jane Hodges, got married and after the church service, the reception was held in a marquee at the family home, The Hollins in Middleton, Ilkley.

'The day ended in a macabre tragedy with the murders of the father, the mother and the brother of the bride; also, the rape of the bride's sister, Amy Hodges. She was the only member of the family, apart from Jane, who had gone on her honeymoon, to survive the slaughter.

'The person responsible for these three murders and the rape of Amy Hodges, the Crown submit, is this defendant, Arthur Mallinson.

'He got into the house by sliding open a patio door which, by pure chance, was left unlocked. He may have been disturbed by the arrival of the family. For whatever reason, he stabbed to death Gordon Hodges on the staircase; Amelia Hodges in her bedroom and he slit the throat of David Hodges in his bedroom causing his death as he lay on his bed.

'Mallinson then entered the bedroom of Amy Hodges. He made her walk down the stairs, through her father's blood, and into the marquee where he handcuffed her and raped her. He drank champagne from a half-consumed bottle left there by the caterers, leaving his fingerprints on the bottle. Mallinson then ordered Amy to take him to the kitchen where he ate some cheese from the refrigerator. He left his unique teeth marks in the cheese.

'Next, he made Amy return to her bedroom where he took off the handcuffs and her nightdress and he raped her again. He stayed with her, talking, until six o'clock in the morning.

'The events are so spine-chilling as to be incapable of belief. But tragically, submit the Crown, it is the truth.

'Your task is to try this defendant on the evidence you will hear, not on what I say to you now and not on prejudice or emotion. Try to put aside the horror of the events and ask yourselves is it proved, say that you are sure that Arthur Mallinson was responsible for these murders and this rape?

'That is all I say at this stage. Mr Oldroyd and I will now call the evidence before you.'

Mr Oldroyd, junior counsel for the Crown, then stood and said: 'My Lord, the prosecution calls Ian Weatherhead.'

A middle-aged man wearing a jacket and tie, which looked as though they only came out on Sundays and holy days, walked into court and into the witness box. He took the oath and stood to face Mr Oldroyd.

'Your full name please?' asked Mr Oldroyd.

'Ian Weatherhead.'

'And are you a marquee erector for Phillip Jones and Sons of Wakefield?'

'Yes, I am.'

'Did you, on the 21st of September this year, together with your son, Richard, erect a marquee at The Hollins, Middleton, Ilkley?'

'I did.'

'And did you return to that address on the 27th of September to take it down?'

'I did.'

'At 6:30 a.m. were you beginning to do that when your attention was drawn to something?'

'Yes, that's true.'

'What was it that attracted your attention?

'A young woman who appeared at the entrance of the marquee.'

'How did she look?'

'Distraught, crying, sobbing. She was wearing a nightgown that looked blood-stained.'

'So, what did you do?'

'I called to her to come and sit down, so she did. I got a chair for her and a couple for me and our Richard. I asked her what was the matter and she told us her whole family had been murdered and she'd been raped. She said the bodies were in the house. I was totally gob-smacked and thought can this really be happening?'

'Did you send your son, Richard, over to the house to investigate?'

'Yes, I did. He went into the house and came back looking ashen. He said it was true and that there were three dead bodies in the house. Then he ran out of the marquee, I assume to be sick.'

'And did you call the police?'

'Yes, 999.'

'Did the girl stay with you while you waited for the police?'

'Yes.'

'And did she talk to you while you waited?'

'No. We asked her if she'd like some tea and she said yes so we poured her some out of our flask.'

'How long was it before the police arrived?'

'It was about ten or fifteen minutes later that uniformed police arrived and about half an hour after them, the C.I.D. came.'

'Thank you, Mr Weatherhead. Please stay there. My learned friend may have some questions for you.'

'Any questions, Mr Mountfield?' asked the judge.

'One, My Lord, thank you,' said Mr Mountfield. 'How would you react if your father, mother and brother had been murdered?'

'Devastated, as she was,' replied Mr Weatherhead.

'No more questions.'

Ian Weatherhead retired.

'My Lord, I call Richard Weatherhead, the son of the last witness,' said Mr Oldroyd.

Richard entered the court, anxiously looking around him. He took the oath and faced Mr Oldroyd.

'Your full name?'

'Richard Weatherhead.'

'Are you the son of the last witness?'

'Yes, I am.'

'And were you and he in the process of dismantling the marquee at The Hollins, Ilkley, on the 27th September?'

'Yes, I was.'

'And did a young lady appear at the entrance to the marquee at about 6:30 a.m.?'

'Yes,'

'Did she say her family had been murdered?'

'She did.'

'And did your father send you to investigate?'

'He did. The French doors to the garden were open, so I went into the house. I saw the body of an old man on the stairs.

I was right shocked.'

'Did you look elsewhere?'

'Yes, I went upstairs, past the body of the man, avoiding him and the blood on a step. I found two more bodies in separate bedrooms. I rushed back to tell Dad and then went to be sick in the marquee toilets.'

'Did you hear Amy, the young lady, say anything else?'

'No.'

'No more questions, My Lord,' said Oldroyd.

'No questions, thank you,' said Mountfield.

Richard Weatherhead then left court.

Beecroft stood and said: 'I call Amy Hodges.'

There was a complete hush as, after a minute or so, young Amy Hodges entered court with her Aunt Violet. Amy went into the witness box and Violet sat near to her on a chair provided by the usher who also gave Amy a glass of water and a box of tissues.

The judge asked Amy if she would prefer to sit when giving evidence, but she said she would stand. She then took the oath on the Testament and faced Mr Beecroft. There was total silence in court. Turnbull thought he would be able to hear a pin drop. The silence was broken by a juror's cough.

'What is your full name?'

'Amy Rosalind Hodges.'

'Were your parents Gordon and Amelia Hodges?'

'Yes, they were.'

'And was your brother David Hodges?'

'Yes, he was.'

'On the 26th September 2008 did your sister, Jane Hodges, marry George Waterhouse?'

'Yes, she did.'

'And, after the wedding ceremony, was the reception held

in a marquee at the family home, The Hollins, Middleton, Ilkley?'

'Yes.'

'And if you look at the photographs in *Divider 2* in the bundle before you, do you see a picture of the marquee?'

'I do, yes.'

'Members of the jury,' said Beecroft. 'You have a bundle in a ring binder before you, one between two. Would you like to open it at *Divider 2*?' The jurors did so and one could see the wonder on their faces at the opulence of the marquee on the beautiful lawn at the side of the house.

'What happened after the wedding reception?'

'At about half past nine, Mummy, Daddy and David left to go to Aunt Violet and Uncle Ronnie's house. I stayed behind because I felt tired.'

'What were you intending to do?'

'Have a shower, read and go to sleep. It had been a long day. I was Matron of Honour and my feet were killing me.'

'Did you shower and read?'

'Yes.'

'What time did you turn the light out?'

'About half past ten.'

'And then what happened?'

'I woke when I heard Mummy screaming and shouting: *Take it all but leave us alone.'*

'What time was that?'

'I don't know.'

'Did you hear anything else?'

'Yes, voices on the stairs. Daddy's and another man's. Daddy was screaming. I thought I must be dreaming and I curled up in a ball.'

'And then?'

'A man came into my bedroom. He told me to turn the light on. I did and then I saw him. He was dirty, unshaven with long, spiky, greasy hair. I'll never forget his face. He was smirking. He was wearing flared trousers and a white T-shirt.'

'Was he holding anything?'

'Yes, a knife like a sheath knife.'

'Will you look at the artist's impression, which is in the bundle under *Divider 3,* and tell me if that's what the man looked like.'

Amy did as instructed and then looked at Mr Beecroft. 'Yes, I did this with Max, the police artist, and that's what the man looked like.'

'Members of the jury,' said Beecroft. 'Please look at *Divider 3.*'

The jurors looked at the artist's impression and then at the dock, no doubt to see if the accused's appearance tallied with the artist's impression.

Amy turned away and took a sip of water. The judge asked: 'Amy, are you all right to continue or do you want a break?'

'No thank you, I'll carry on, My Lord.'

'Amy, tell us what happened next,' said Beecroft.

'He came over to me. Then I noticed how much he smelt of BO, stale sweat. He was unshaven, dirty, disgusting.'

'Did he do or say anything?'

'He held the knife to my throat. I could see blood on it. He said: *Scream and you're dead.* I was tempted. I tried to scream, but nothing came out.'

'And next?'

'He told me to go with him down to the marquee.'

'And did you?'

'Yes. It was dark. There was only the light from my bedroom, but I groped my way down the stairs in front of him. I felt something on my feet, something wet. I didn't see Daddy's body. I was just in a daze.'

'Did you enter the marquee?'

'Yes, he walked me out of the French doors and through the tented tunnel into the marquee. He told me to turn the lights on, which I did at the master switch near the entrance, so the marquee was a blaze of light. Then he pushed me to the far end where he handcuffed me with my arms at the front. I begged him not to kill me and he said he wouldn't if I did as he said. He said: *That's where your mother went wrong.* He went across the marquee and drank some champagne from a half empty bottle.'

'Did you have any?'

'No. Then he pushed me to the floor. I was in a full-length nightdress. He lifted it up and got on top of me. He said he wouldn't kill me, he just wanted to fuck me.'

'What did he do?'

'He penetrated me. It hurt, but I didn't resist because I was terrified.'

'Were you still handcuffed?'

'Yes.'

'What next?'

'He asked where the kitchen was. I said I would show him. We walked out of the marquee and into the house. I turned the lights on and we went down the hall and into the kitchen where he ate some cheese from the refrigerator whilst I just sat there trembling.'

'What next?'

'He led me back upstairs. I think it was then that he took my handcuffs off. He pulled my nightdress off over my head and then he penetrated me again. I don't know if he came either time. Then he started talking to me as if I was his girlfriend.

It was weird. He said he was on the run. He had avoided being seen by the police.'

'Were you on any contraceptive device?'

'No,' she said, 'the doctor later gave me a morning-after pill. I was a virgin.'

Dead silence and a pause.

'How long did he stay after that?'

'A few hours. I couldn't understand why. He kept talking. I think his accent was Geordie. He kept telling me not to knock his leg because it was injured. He told me not to go into any of the other bedrooms. He finally said he was going. He tied me up, my hands and feet, with laces. I don't know where they came from. It was nearly daylight. Then he was gone. He took the handcuffs with him.'

'Did you free yourself?'

'Yes.'

'How?'

'By struggling free. It took me some time.'

'What time was it by now?'

'About 6:30 or 7:00 a.m.'

'Did you hear anyone?'

'After a while I heard noises from the marquee.'

'Did you go down to the marquee?'

'Yes.'

'Did you walk past your father?'

'Yes, he was dead. I went back upstairs into Mummy's bedroom and David's. They were both dead. Then I went over to the marquee.'

'Did you speak to the marquee men?'

'Yes, I did.'

'Finally, two things, if I may. Did you later discover items were missing?'

'Yes, my mother's Cartier watch and her diamond necklace. She always wore them. The watch was a present from my Dad for their silver wedding and he bought the necklace for her in India where they went for a holiday.'

'Would you look at this watch, exhibit four.' The usher showed the witness the watch recovered from Mr Hardcastle's shop.

'Yes, this is my mother's, or one identical to it.' It was then passed round the jury before being handed back to the usher.

'Will you look at this necklace, exhibit five.' The usher handed her the necklace recovered from Fred Hardcastle's shop.

'Yes, this is my mother's. My father bought it for her in India.' It was then passed round the jury before being handed back to the usher.

'Secondly, did you go to your mother's body and touch her at all?'

'No, no. I couldn't bear to touch her.'

'Finally, did you have any injuries?'

'Yes, my wrists were scratched from trying to get free from the cuffs and laces.'

'Thank you. I have no more questions.'

The judge turned to Amy: 'I think that's enough for today. Your aunt will take you to her home. Try to get some rest, but please resist the temptation to talk to your aunt about your evidence. You are still in the witness box and not permitted to talk to anyone about your evidence until it is concluded. Do you understand?'

'Yes,' replied Amy.

'We will adjourn now until ten-thirty tomorrow morning.'

The jury filed out and then the judge retired. Amy sat in court with her aunt until the court had been cleared. Turnbull and Jasper went outside for some fresh air. Amy was brought out by her aunt and a policewoman and went straight to a waiting car.

'I thought she did very well,' said Turnbull.

'Yes, so did I,' said Jasper.

'What matters is how she handles cross-examination,' said Turnbull. 'Let's hope she gets a good night's rest.'

Turnbull and Jasper went back to HQ and then to the local pub popular with the police. Turnbull bought them a pint each.

'Is there anything else we need to be doing?' said Turnbull.

'Not that I can think of,' replied Jasper.

'It's out of our hands now. It's odd that he didn't leave her handcuffed,' said Turnbull.

'I disagree,' said Jasper. 'He couldn't say she consented if he'd left her cuffed.'

'That's true.'

Chapter 15

The court reassembled at 10:30 the following morning. As usual, the public gallery was packed, as was the press gallery. This was the day they had been waiting for. The ghouls loved to see the complainant in a rape trial being taken apart.

Amy came into court with her aunt and they both sat down near the witness box. Amy was wearing a white blouse, black skirt and flat shoes. The usher placed a glass of water and a box of tissues in the witness box for her. A hush descended on the court as the jury came in and sat down.

'All rise,' called the court clerk.

The judge came into court and bowed to counsel who bowed in return.

Amy went into the witness box and stood anxiously awaiting the ordeal.

Mr Mountfield stood and said: 'May it please you Lordship.' He turned to Amy.

'How long was the man with you in all?'

'About seven hours.'

'Can we please look together at the CCTV recording?' A screen came down from the ceiling opposite the jury, which was visible to all. A projector followed and the recording was played showing a man at the patio door and the door opening.

When the recording finished, Mountfield asked: 'How did this man get into your house?'

'I assume through the patio door.'

'So, it was unlocked?'

'Yes.'

'Your parents were security conscious were they not?'

'Yes.'

'They have installed a CCTV system?'

'Yes.'

'The gates are controlled and cannot be opened without the householder, or someone in the house, pressing a button inside the house to open the gates. Is that correct?'

'Yes,'

'And there is no way into the grounds other than through the main gates?'

'That is true.'

'How is it that he got into the grounds?'

'I don't know.

'You opened the gate for him?'

'No.'

'How is it that this patio door was left unlocked?'

'The catch didn't work properly.'

'For how long had it been like that?'

'Several days.'

'Was anyone contacted to put it right?'

'No, my father was going to do it but didn't get around to it with all the fuss over the wedding.'

'How had it been damaged?'

'I don't know. Are you sure it won't lock?'

'Yes, I'm pretty sure.'

Turnbull wondered whether the defence team had checked it. He wondered what was coming next.

'How many doors are there providing access to the house?'

'About seven.' The jury looked visibly surprised.

'And the man just happened to find the only one which was unlocked.'

'Yes.'

'Are you sure you didn't let him in? Just watch the CCTV

recording again.'

The court watched the recording again.

'How is it possible to slide this door open from the outside?'

'If it's slightly ajar you can get your fingers in and open it.'

'But it has to be slightly ajar for that to be possible?

'Yes.'

Mountfield continued: 'If the window is in its proper place when properly shut, locked or unlocked, it is not possible to open it from the outside?'

'No. I'm not sure.'

'And no one in the house seems to have noticed that this door had been left ajar?'

'No.'

'Tell me, why were you the only member of the family to stay behind?'

Turnbull sighed in relief. Mountfield was moving on to another topic.

'I've told you. I was tired.'

'How old are you?'

'Nineteen.'

'You weren't the worse for drink?'

'No.'

'The evening out was a continuation of the family celebration?'

'Yes.'

'I suggest you stayed behind because you had arranged for Arthur Mallinson to come to your house after the others had gone out.'

'That is ridiculous.'

'And you let him in by opening the patio door from the inside?'

'No.'

'Do you know there are no fingerprints on the outside of the door?'

'I've been told.'

'Had you been in town on the night before the wedding?'

'Yes.'

'With other girls?'

'Yes.'

'In a pub?'

'Yes.'

'And you met Mallinson, I suggest, in the White Horse pub?'

'That is rubbish. How dare you suggest that?'

'I dare because it is Arthur Mallinson's case that you deliberately stayed at home so that you could let him into the house, which is what you did.'

'No. I was tired, so I decided to stay at home.'

'And I suggest you had consensual sex with him when he arrived at your house by invitation?'

'No, that's nonsense.'

'And he left the house before your family returned.'

'No.'

'And I put it to you that you are now suggesting he committed the murders and raped you because you are ashamed, in retrospect, of having allowed him to come to the house to have sex with you?'

'No, that's complete and utter nonsense.'

'And I suggest you got your mother's blood on your nightgown because you went to tend to her after she was murdered, not by Mallinson, but by a different person who came into the house after he had left.'

'No.'

'Is it your evidence that seeing your mother's body, you

never even touched her?'

'Yes.'

'And I suggest you got your father's blood on your right foot when you went to tend to him well after Mallinson had left.'

'No, that is wrong.'

'And I suggest you self-inflicted the scratches on your wrists so that you could suggest you'd been handcuffed.'

'No, that's absurd.'

'You allege, Miss Hodges, you were raped and yet there is no sign whatsoever, is there, of injury to your private parts?'

'I was terrified. I thought that if I resisted, he would kill me.'

'As I understand your evidence, he handcuffed you in the marquee.'

'Yes.'

'Yet, upstairs, he took the handcuffs off.'

'Yes.'

'And when he left he tied your wrists with laces and took the handcuffs with him.'

Yes.'

'Did he say why he didn't cuff you again?'

'No.'

'I suggest you have to say he handcuffed you only once and tied your wrists with laces the second time to explain the fact there were no handcuffs left behind?'

'No.'

'And the laces, where are the laces?'

'I don't know.'

'Well, after you had released yourself from them, did you dispose of them?'

'No.'

'Well, then, they should still be there in your bedroom.'

'Yes.'

'And yet they have disappeared?'

'Yes, it seems so.'

'You are lying, are you not?'

'No.'

'I have no more questions,' said Mr Mountfield.

The judge addressed Mr Beecroft: 'Have you any re-examination of this witness?'

'No, My Lord, thank you.'

The judge said: 'We will have a break for thirty minutes.'

The judge and jury left court. Amy went out, accompanied by her aunt.

The press made a beeline for the door. Turnbull could imagine what a field day they would have with that cross-examination. He made a mental note to buy the *Yorkshire Evening Post* and the Bradford *Telegraph and Argus* when he left court.

Turnbull went to the police room, waited a while and then rang Amy who had by then arrived back at Violet's home: 'Amy, when you went to the White Horse pub the night before the wedding, you say you met girlfriends there. How many?' he asked.

'Oh, three. They were all to be bridesmaids the following day. We were all really jolly.'

'Can I have their names?'

'Yes, Georgina Stewart, Amy Feather and Hermione Gough.'

'Have you got their contact numbers?'

'Yes, they're on my phone. Just a minute I'll give them to you.'

Amy then dictated the three mobile numbers to Turnbull.

'I'll speak to them. You think they'll confirm that you never spoke to a strange man when you were in the pub that night?'

'I'm sure they will. It was all girls' talk. The last thing we were thinking of was men.'

'Do you think it possible that Mallinson was in the pub?'

'I have no idea. He could have been there I suppose, but I certainly never spoke to him or noticed him. If I did, I'd have recognised him when he came into my room.'

'Fair enough. There's nothing else I need to speak to you about.'

'Turnbull returned to headquarters and called Jane Rowley into his office: 'Jane, I want you to contact these three girls. They met Amy at the White Horse pub in Ilkley the night before the wedding, i.e. on the 25th September, a Thursday. I want you to ask them whether they saw Amy having any verbal contact with a forty-five-year-old man.'

'Will do,' said Jane.

Chapter 16

Jane went straight to her telephone in the C.I.D. room. It was noisy. About a dozen detective constables were there, some talking, some typing, but all looking very busy. Her and Crawford's desks were in the murder squad corner. DS Roberts' and Jasper's desks were elsewhere.

Jane got through to Georgina Stewart's mobile: 'I'm Detective Jane Rowley of the Bradford Homicide Unit. We are investigating the murders of the Hodges family and an allegation of rape of Amy Hodges. Were you in the White Horse pub in Ilkley on the night before the wedding?'

'Yes, the bridesmaids were there with Amy who was to be maid of honour. We were chatting about our duties and things in general, you know, girls' talk,' replied Georgina.

'Did a man speak to Amy?'

'Not that I remember. What do you mean?'

'Well, did a man in his forties come over and chat to Amy?'

'Not that I remember. No, I'm sure not. She stayed with us the whole time.'

'I'll need a statement from you to that effect. Can you come to Bradford Police Headquarters and do that for me ASAP please?'

'Yes, of course,' said Georgina. 'I work in Bradford, so I'll call in my lunch hour if that's okay?'

'Excellent,' said Jane. 'Come to reception and ask for me and I'll come down and meet you. By the way, do you know where Amy Feather and Hermione Gough are?'

'Yes, they're abroad on holiday.'

Shucks, thought Jane, *we should have made this enquiry earlier.*

* * *

Jane reported to Turnbull what she had learned and he said he would pass the information on to Beecroft as he might want to apply to call Georgina in the rebuttal of Mallinson's suggestion, of which they had no notice until Mountfield cross-examined Amy, that he met Amy in the pub.

* * *

Everyone returned to court after thirty minutes, save for a substantial number of the reporters who were no doubt telephoning their reports through to their editors.

'My Lord, the prosecution's next witness is Professor John Talbot.'

Professor Talbot walked into the witness box and took the oath. He had an air of authority about him which Turnbull greatly admired.

'I am John Edward Talbot, Professor of Forensic Pathology at the University of Leeds.'

'Did you, on the 27th of September of this year, go to The Hollins, Middleton, Ilkley?'

'I did.'

'For what purpose?'

'I was told there were bodies there for me to examine.'

'And were there?'

'Yes, the bodies of Gordon Hodges, Amelia Hodges and Richard Hodges.'

'Did you form an assessment as to how they died?'

'Yes, Gordon and Amelia had been stabbed through the heart and Richard's throat had been cut.'

'Did you arrange for the bodies to be taken to Leeds City Morgue?'

'Yes.'

'And did you there perform post mortem examinations?'

'Yes, I did.'

'Did they confirm your initial conclusions?'

'Yes, Gordon was stabbed repeatedly in the heart by a single-edged Bowie-type of knife with a four-inch one-sided blade. Amelia, likewise, had been stabbed repeatedly in the chest with a single-edged Bowie-type of knife with a four-inch one-sided blade. They were upward thrusts and, from the tracks, I assess they were inflicted by a right-handed man.'

'And David?' asked Beecroft.

'David's throat was cut, but I can't say with, or by, what type of knife, save that it had a sharp blade. Nor can I say whether the knife was held in the left or right hand.'

'Did you examine Amy Hodges together with the Police Surgeon, Doctor John Carr?'

Yes, we examined her together. She had seven roughly parallel transverse abrasions encircling her left wrist. The longest were two centimetres and the shortest six millimetres. On the right wrist were four similar abrasions. They were consistent with being handcuffed or bound by the wrists and the victim struggling to free herself.'

'What else did you find?'

'The sole of her right foot was caked in blood which was seeping, or had seeped, between her toes.'

'What about her private parts?'

'There was no fresh injury at all. She complained of pain in the lower abdomen, but I found nothing to account for that.'

'What was her state generally?'

'Beside herself with grief.'

'No more questions,' said Beecroft.

'Any cross-examination, Mr Mountfield?' asked the judge.

'Yes, My Lord, one. The wrist marks. Were any handcuffs left at the scene?'

'No, not so far as I am aware.'

'Or any laces?'

'No.'

'Thank you,' said Mountfield.

'I think we'll call it a day,' said the judge. 'Ten-thirty tomorrow morning please.'

The jurors filed out.

'All rise,' said the court clerk. And the judge withdrew.

Turnbull went to the local newsvendor and bought the first edition of the *Telegraph & Argus* and the *Yorkshire Evening Post*. The *Post*'s front page led with the words *NO, NO, NO* referring to Amy's response to the suggestions in cross-examination. The editorial ran an article about the cruel way the defence had been conducted, asking *Why was this permitted?*

When Turnbull got back to his office, he switched on his computer and looked at the *Evening Standard*. It carried an article by John Mortimer, Q.C. saying that defence counsel had no alternative but to put his client's case. How much worse would it have been if Mallinson himself had cross-examined Amy?

Turnbull hoped that the jury would obey that judge's direction not to read the press or watch television reports of the case. He wondered how Amy had taken it. He rang her Aunt Violet's home, only to be told that Amy had shut herself in her bedroom.

'I will come to see her, if she wishes,' said Turnbull.

'That's very kind of you,' said Violet. 'But I am taking her to Majorca tomorrow for a few days' sunshine.'

'I would delay that until the trial is over, just in case Amy is required again.'

'All right, if we must. Please let me know when we can go.'

'Will do,' said Turnbull. 'Give her my best wishes.'

'Thank you, I will do that. Bye.'

At last her ordeal is over, thought Turnbull. *Everything should be straightforward from now on.*

Little did he know.

Chapter 17

The following morning, the court reassembled. Mr Beecroft stood and called the next witness, Fred Hardcastle.

A rather nervous-looking man walked into court. He had the same appearance as that shown to Jane Rowley, rather sleazy with greasy, greying hair swept backwards. He took the oath and stood facing Mr Beecroft.

'Your full name.'

'Frederick Hardcastle.'

'Your occupation.'

'Jeweller.'

'Does the witness need a warning?' asked the judge of Beecroft.

'No, My Lord, I think not. Mr Hardcastle has been told that in all circumstances he will not be prosecuted for handling stolen goods,' said Beecroft.

'Very well,' said the judge. 'Carry on.'

'Mr Hardcastle, please would you look at these two items of jewellery.'

He was shown the Cartier watch and the diamond necklace, exhibits 4 and 5.

'Do you recognise these?' asked Beecroft.

'Yes, I do. I bought them on the 27th of September.'

'From whom?'

'A man who came into my shop in Skipton.'

'Had you met this man before?'

'Not so far as I am aware.'

'Where did he say he had got them?'

'He said they were his mother's and that she'd died and he

needed to raise some money to pay for her funeral.'

'Did you believe him?'

'No, they were of exquisite quality and he didn't look like the sort of bloke whose mother would have jewellery like that.'

'Did you realise at once that they were stolen?'

'Yes, I did.'

'Did you buy them?'

'Yes, I gave him £600 for the watch and £200 for the necklace.'

'In cash?'

'Yes.'

'Did you record the sale?'

'No, nor the purchase.'

'On the Monday following, did Detective Constable Jane Rowley and Detective Constable Jonathan Crawford come into your shop saying they wished to buy a watch?'

'They did. They were pretending to be an engaged couple, not police officers.'

'After you had shown them the watch, did they then disclose that they were police officers and state that you had bought recently stolen jewellery?'

'They did.'

'Did you later attend a VIPER identification parade, that's a video identification parade electronic recording, at Bradford Police Headquarters?'

'I did.'

'And from the photographs shown to you, were you able to pick out the person who sold the jewellery to you?'

'Yes, I picked out number five.'

'My Lord, the defence admit that the defendant's photograph was number five of the twelve shown.'

'Is that correct, Mr Mountfield?' asked the judge.

'Yes, My Lord.'

'Members of the jury,' said the judge. 'One way to admit evidence is by admission. You can take it that Mallinson's photograph was amongst the twelve shown and was number five.'

'I have no more questions,' said Mr Beecroft.

Mr Mountfield stood to cross-examine: 'Mr Hardcastle, do you believe you would recognise the seller if you saw him in person?'

'I think so, I picked him out in the photos shown me. I was pretty sure it was him.'

'Mr Hardcastle, I am going to ask you to look at another man, this time in person, to see if he was the man who sold the jewellery to you. It's not the number five you previously identified.'

Mr Beecroft rose to his feet: 'My Lord, I wish to raise an objection in the absence of the jury.'

The judge turned to the jury: 'I am the judge of the law and procedure. You are the judges of the facts. I decide matters of law in your absence, so if you would kindly retire to your jury room, we will let you know when to return.'

The jury left court, as did Fred Hardcastle who was taken to the witness room.

The judge addressed Mr Beecroft: 'Yes, Mr Beecroft?'

'My Lord, my learned friend says that he is going to bring into court one person who I believe he is going to suggest is the one who sold Mr Hardcastle the jewellery. Such a procedure is contrary to all the rules relating to identification evidence. It is like a witness pointing to the dock and saying *That is the man;* a dock identification. It draws attention to one person, not as it should be done, asking the witness whether he can pick out a person from an identification parade, whether live or by photograph. That, My Lord, is my submission.'

'Yes, Mr Mountfield?' said the judge.

'My Lord, my learned friend is talking about prosecution evidence of identification. The rules relating to identification evidence bear no relation to a defence case. I am only seeking to cast doubt on the prosecution case, not, as the prosecution do, to prove guilt. The defence do not have the facilities to conduct an identification parade,' said Mountfield. 'That is my submission.'

'Thank you both,' said the judge. 'I rule that the question can be asked. Please bring the jury back.'

The jury file back into court and Fred Hardcastle returned to the witness box. Turnbull thought *What's coming next?*

'Yes, Mr Mountfield,' said the judge.

'Mr Hardcastle, would you kindly look at the gentleman who will now come into court and tell me, after he has retired, whether you recognise him.'

A man walked into court, stood for a few seconds and then withdrew. Turnbull immediately recognised the man as Bill Patterson who had been to his office to admit the murders and whom he had dismissed as a fraud. Turnbull looked at the back of the court and there saw Captain Clarke with a broad grin on his face.

That bastard Clarke, thought Turnbull, *he's set up Patterson to come and admit the murders and say he, not Mallinson, sold the jewellery to Hardcastle. And he's got at Hardcastle to go along with that set up. I'll make sure Bob Hewitt makes Hardcastle's life miserable from hereon.*

After Patterson had withdrawn, Mountfield asked Hardcastle whether or not he recognised the man?

'Yes, I believe he was the man who sold me the jewellery.'

A distinct murmur arose in court whilst those present

absorbed the implication of that answer. Would the jury now think it possible that two men entered The Hollins that night; Mallinson who had sex with Amy and Patterson who came later and committed the murders and stole the jewellery? Suddenly, the defence seemed to have fresh legs.

'So, Mr Hardcastle, are you now saying you can't be sure which of the two men sold you the jewellery?'

'No, I now think it was the second man.'

'Why say then, at the VIPER identification parade, it was number five?'

'I don't know.'

'Has anyone spoken to you about your evidence since the VIPER parade?'

'No.'

Oh, yes, pigs might fly, thought Turnbull.

'No more questions,' said Mountfield.

That was bad, thought Turnbull. All he could hope for was that the jury would think Hardcastle was bent and that he'd been got at.

Mr Beecroft stood to re-examine Mr Hardcastle: 'You understand you are in a court of law and that this evidence is very important and you have taken an oath to tell only the truth?'

'Yes, sir.'

'You said you believed that the man who came into court was the man who sold you the jewellery.'

'Yes, I did, but I can't be certain. I have a lot of customers.'

'Whereas, at the VIPER parade, you identified number five as that person. You have thus changed your account. Why?'

'When the second man came into court, I saw him in person, not in a photo, I thought I'd made a mistake at the parade. I'm sorry.'

'I have no more question,' said Beecroft.

There followed, in the wake of Hardcastle's evidence, a tranche of evidence which was not in dispute; the scientific evidence as to fingerprints and blood stains; the police evidence as to the search for, the arrest and interview of Mallinson; the taking of samples from Mallinson; and the greenkeeper's evidence of disturbing Mallinson in the rain shelter.

'Is that the conclusion of the prosecution's case?' asked the judge of Beecroft.

'My Lord, we have potentially more witnesses who are not available until tomorrow morning,' said Beecroft.

'Very well, we'll adjourn until tomorrow morning at ten o'clock,' said the judge. 'Mr Mountfield, can you tell me whether you intend calling your client?'

'Yes, My Lord, and additional witnesses.'

Oh boy, thought Turnbull, *we're going to hear Patterson admitting the murders. Who thought there would be no hitches?*

Turnbull left court in a hurry. He had a job for Jane Rowley. He told Beecroft and Oldroyd that he would join them shortly and went to phone Jane from court.

'Things aren't going that well here,' he said. 'I want you to go to The Hollins and try the patio door. We've assumed Amy is right about the catch on the door not working properly, so that Mallinson could gain entry. But, stupidly, I haven't checked whether that's correct. Please go to the house and try it. I'll ring you on your mobile in an hour.'

'Will do,' said Jane. 'I'm sorry I didn't think of that before.'

So am I, thought Turnbull. She rang off.

Turnbull and Jasper then went back to the prosecution conference room. Beecroft, Oldroyd and Gibson were still there.

'Well, well,' said Beecroft. 'That was a turn up for the books. I assume they will be calling Patterson to confess to the murders. Please get a transcript of what he said to you when he came to confess and have copies available for the witness box, the jury and the judge. Who else are they calling?'

'I've no idea,' said Turnbull.

'Well,' said Beecroft. 'We can only wait and see.'

'We have traced one of the girls in the pub,' said Turnbull. 'She says no way did Amy chat up a forty-five-year-old man.'

'Excellent,' said Beecroft. 'We'll call her first thing tomorrow.'

'I have another enquiry ongoing,' said Turnbull. 'I'll let you know what the result is in the morning.'

'Come on, Dave, let's go to the pub.'

Turnbull and Jasper left and went to Jacob's Well. A fire was lit and the pub was quiet, just as they liked it.

'What was looking like a cast-iron case is beginning to show weakness,' said Turnbull as he and Jasper took a sip of their beers. 'Have you seen anyone outside court, waiting to give evidence, whom you recognise as a potential defence witness?'

'No,' said Jasper.

'Well, we'll just have to deal with things on the hoof. Let's hope Georgina Stewart's good. I'll ring Jane.'

He caught her just as she was examining the door.

'What have you found?' he asked.

'Well, I can see what Amy was getting at. The catch is very difficult to engage but, with a lot of force, it is possible to lock the patio door. Sorry for the bad news,' she replied.

Turnbull rang off and told Jasper that it was possible to lock the patio door.

'Oh, Christ,' said Jasper.

'I couldn't put it better myself,' said Turnbull.

Chapter 18

The following morning, at 9:30, Turnbull went to the robing room to find Beecroft.

'Last night, I got Jane to try the patio door. I should have thought of it before. She says that with a lot of force, the door can be locked.'

'Oh, Lord,' said Beecroft.

I couldn't put it better myself, thought Turnbull.

The court reassembled at 10:00 a.m.

Beecroft stood to address the judge in the absence of the jury: 'My Lord, you will remember that during his cross-examination of Amy Hodges, Mr Mountfield suggested the accused had met Amy at the White Horse public house, on the evening before the wedding, when she was with three or four other girls.

'This is the first we had heard of that suggestion. We have traced one of the girls who was with Amy.

'I now hand to you her statement which I now formally serve on my learned friend for the defence in a notice of additional evidence. We intend calling her now to give evidence for the Crown.'

The judge and defence counsel read the statement. The judge addressed Mr Mountfield: 'Have you any observations, Mr Mountfield?'

'It's a bit late, My Lord,' replied Mountfield.

'Only because your suggestion came late,' said the judge. 'No, I shall allow the evidence. Let the jury return.'

Beecroft said nothing about not disclosing to the defence about the catch on the door which could be locked. He obviously thought it was up to the defence to check it themselves. Turnbull wasn't certain about the propriety of that decision but Beecroft was in charge. It was his decision. If it had been Turnbull's decision, he would have disclosed the discovery to the defence.

The jury filed into court.

Beecroft rose and said: 'The Crown calls Georgina Stewart.'

An attractive, tall young woman walked confidently into court and into the witness box. She took the oath on the Testament and turned to face Beecroft.

'What is your full name?'

'Georgina Alice Stewart.'

'And your occupation?'

'I am doing articles to become a solicitor.'

Yes, thought Turnbull, *things are getting better.*

'Were you a bridesmaid at Jane Hodges' wedding?'

'Yes, I was.'

'And was Amy Hodges the Matron of Honour?'

'Yes, she was.'

'Did you see Amy the night before the wedding?'

'Yes, myself and the other two bridesmaids met her at the White Horse pub in Ilkley.'

'At any time did Amy talk to anyone outside your group of four?'

'No, we were chatting avidly about the wedding and what our duties were, etcetera. She didn't speak to anyone else.'

'Thank you, Miss Stewart. Stay there, please, as my learned friend may have some questions.'

'Yes, thank you,' said Mountfield as he rose to his feet.

'How long were you in the pub?'

'About two hours.'

'From when to when?'

'From eight-thirty, our meeting time, until closing time at ten-thirty.'

'Did you not go to the toilet during those two hours?'

'Yes, but not for long.'

'And were you with Amy throughout?'

'Yes, it was girly talk.'

'I suggest you weren't watching her the whole time.'

'Yes, I was.'

'And I suggest that at one point, a man came over and spoke to Amy for about thirty minutes.'

'No. That never happened.'

'Thank you, no more questions,' said Mountfield.

'My Lord, that is the case for the Crown,' said Beecroft, meaning that the prosecution had now closed its case. Next, it was the turn of the defence.

'Now, Mr Mountfield, are you ready to present your case?'

'Yes,' replied Mountfield.

'We'll have a break for fifteen minutes,' said the judge.

The judge and the jury withdrew. Turnbull and Jasper remained in court until it reassembled.

* * *

'Yes, Mr Mountfield,' said the judge.

'May it please your Lordship, I call Arthur Mallinson to give evidence in his own defence.'

Mallinson, not handcuffed, left the dock and walked to the witness box with a prison officer in front of him and one behind. He took the oath.

He looked, to Turnbull, very respectable for a change. He was wearing what looked like a new single-breasted suit, a white shirt, blue striped tie and black shoes. His hair was neatly cut and he was clean shaven. *Quite a transformation,* thought Turnbull, *I wonder where he got that suit?* Captain Clarke was still smiling. *He knows the answer,* thought Turnbull.

Mallinson took the oath in a measured tone.

'What is your full name?' asked Mountfield.

'Arthur Mallinson.'

'And your occupation?'

'I'm unemployed at present due to being held in custody since my arrest.'

'Mr Mallinson, did you murder the three members of the Hodges family?'

'Most certainly not.'

'Did you, before the 26th of September, meet Amy Hodges?'

'Yes, I did, on the evening of the 25th of September.'

'Where?'

'In a public house in Ilkley. The White Horse.'

'Did you speak to her?'

'Yes, she was with girlfriends. I was alone and caught her eye. After about ten minutes, I went over to speak to her.'

'About what?'

'Oh, this and that, nothing in particular. She told me her sister was getting married the following day and she was the Maid of Honour. We talked for about half an hour and, by closing time, she'd had a few drinks. Just as the pub was emptying, she asked what I was doing the following evening. I said not a lot and then she said she would be at home alone after the wedding and she asked me if I fancied dropping in for a drink at about ten o'clock. I said I would and she gave me the address. She told me to speak into the intercom at the gate, when I arrived, and she would open the gate to let me in. She told me she'd meet me at the patio window.'

'And did you go to the house the following night, as

arranged?'

'Yes, I did. I was staying at a lodging house in Ilkley. I showered and dressed and got a taxi. It dropped me at the gate. I pressed the button on the intercom and she answered and let me in. I walked up the drive and went to the sliding window on the terrace. I could see Amy through the glass and she opened the window. I didn't touch it. And I went in.

'She asked me if I wanted to go across to the marquee for a drink and she led me out through some French windows, which she unlocked, leading into the tented entrance to the marquee. It was already lit. She asked me if I wanted some champagne. When I said yes, she took me over to a trestle table where there were some half-drunk bottles of champagne and she just told me to help myself, so I did. There weren't any clean glasses, so I just drank straight from the bottle.'

'Did Amy have any champagne?'

'I can't remember. And then she asked me if I wanted anything to eat. I said I'd eaten but some cheese would be nice, so she led me back into the house and into the kitchen. The lights were on and she went to the fridge and took some cheese out. I took a lump of it, took a bite and said it was good.

'We chatted for a while in the kitchen and then she said her parents were out at her aunt and uncle's. She said she was on her own for a change and that's when I thought this was a green light. One of us said: *shall we go upstairs*? And she led the way up to her bedroom.

'She took her nightdress off and she'd nothing on underneath. We made love.'

Turnbull could sense the atmosphere in court at the mention of the word *love*. *What an accomplished liar,* he thought.

'Did you handcuff her?'

'Certainly not.'

'Did you have handcuffs with you?'

'You're joking. No, of course not.'

'How did she get friction marks and abrasions on her wrists?'

'I have no idea. Certainly not from anything I did.'

This is going well for him, thought Turnbull. *He's coming across as a perfectly decent man, contrary to what I know to be the truth.* He felt like standing and shouting: *This is all rubbish.* Turnbull could sense that Jasper felt the same and thought *We should be used to this by now.* But he never found it easy to sit quietly and listen to lie after lie.

'Mr Mallinson, did you force her to have sexual intercourse with you?'

'No, I did not. She was talking and acting perfectly normally.'

'Did you ejaculate?'

'No, I've had a vasectomy, but I did climax and so did she. We chatted for a while and she said *we must meet again, you know where I live.* I said okay. Then she said *you must go before my parents come back, it's been nice meeting you.* And then I left and walked back into Ilkley to the boarding house and went to bed.'

'What time would that be?'

'About eleven or eleven-thirty. The following morning, I went into Ilkley and then had some lunch. The next thing I knew was, in the afternoon, I turned on the telly in my room and there was an artist's impression of me and a reporter saying I was wanted for a triple murder. I couldn't believe it. I hadn't murdered anyone.

'I get claustrophobia. I can't stand being locked up in a confined space. I panicked and immediately left the boarding house and went on the run. The rest you know. I was caught near Lofthouse in North Yorkshire. I didn't murder anyone. I'm innocent.'

Mallinson appeared to shed a tear. *God, what next?* thought Turnbull.

Mountfield said he had no more questions and sat down.

Beecroft stood up to cross-examine.

'Can I start, Mr Mallinson, questioning you from the beginning of your account please?'

'Yes, sir.'

'You committed an offence of burglary of a dwelling house, did you not?'

'Yes, I did.'

'You stole money that had been left on a sideboard in the kitchen?'

'Yes.'

'How did you gain entry into the house?'

'By picking the lock.'

'Had you with you a lock-picking device?'

'Yes, I had.'

'And you were caught, were you not, exiting the building?'

'Yes, it seems I triggered the beam of an invisible alarm.'

'And you were arrested?'

'Yes.'

'And taken to Keighley Police Station where you were kept in custody pending your appearance at the Keighley and Bingley Magistrates' Court in Bingley?'

'Yes.'

'And you were then interviewed?'

'Yes, I was.'

'And, during the interview, you admitted five more burglaries of dwelling houses in Keighley?'

'Yes, I did.'

'All of which you committed by picking locks?'

'Yes, I'm good at it.'

'So, would you describe yourself as a professional house burglar?'

'Mr Mountfield,' said the judge. 'Any objections?'

'No. My Lord, in the circumstances,' replied Mountfield.

'I understand,' said the judge. 'Continue, Mr Beecroft.'

'I repeat, would you describe yourself as a professional house burglar?'

'You could say that, yes.'

'Even though you have no previous convictions?'

'Yes.'

'So, a very successful house burglar?'

'You could say that.'

'And you knew that because of that professionalism, the police were opposing bail when you appeared before the Magistrates' Court?'

'Yes, they told me that.'

'So, you decided to escape?'

'Yes.'

'And you did so by breaking a large window in the holding room?'

'Yes.'

'How did you manage to do that without those outside hearing you?'

'I'm good at it.'

'Where did you learn these skills, Mr Mallinson?'

'In the army.'

'Yes, you were in the army for one year, were you not?'

'Yes, I was.'

'But you were cashiered?'

'Yes, I was.'

'Discharged from the army?'

'You could say that, yes.'

'So, you were outside the Bingley Magistrates' Court, having escaped. Where did you go next?'

'I ran over the moors to Ilkley, through Eldwick and Burley Woodhead.'

'Did you see any police looking for you?'

'Yes, but I kept a low profile.'

'So, again, in a professional way?'

'Yes, you could say that.'

'And when in Ilkley, how did you get money?'

'I robbed a man at a cashpoint on Brook Street.'

The jaws of some of the jurors dropped. *They're now getting a truer picture*, thought Turnbull.

'So, the man was at the cashpoint, putting in his card and when the money appeared, you grabbed it from him?'

'Yes, three hundred quid.'

'Are you sure, Mr Mallinson, you are not making this up to explain how you could, as you allege, pay cash for your lodging house?'

'No.'

'So, according to you, you now have three hundred pounds on you. Did the man raise a hue and cry?'

'You what?'

'Did the man shout *I've been robbed*?'

'Well, I was gone, wasn't I? I hopped it through the car park at the back of Brook Street.'

'And where did you go next?'

'I went to Sunwin House and bought some clothes and toiletries.'

'Did you keep the receipt?'

'No.'

'Going to Sunwin House meant crossing Brook Street where you had just committed a robbery.'

'If you say so.'

'And then?'

'I went looking for a boarding house with a vacancies sign.'

'And you say you found one at 42 The Crescent?'

'Yes.'

'So, when you presented there, you would be hot and sweaty?'

'Yes.'

'With only a Sunwin House bag?'

'Yes.'

'And did you pay cash?'

'Yes, I did. Eighty quid for two nights.'

'Were you not afraid the police would check boarding houses for you, the escaped prisoner?'

'No, you take risks, don't you?'

'And did you sign a register?'

'No. I wasn't asked to.'

'Really, Mr Mallinson, did you not think that was strange?'

'No.'

'You are saying that, I suggest, because you know a handwriting check would reveal that any signature there, would not be yours.'

'No.'

'When you were taken into custody, you had to sign a document acknowledging the items you had in your possession, did you not?'

'Yes, I did.'

'So, the police had your genuine signature, Mr Mallinson.'

'Yes.'

'I suggest that if you stayed at a boarding house, as you

allege, you would have signed a register.'

'Well, I didn't.'

'Why didn't you mention staying at a boarding house when you were arrested?'

'I didn't want to get the proprietors into trouble.'

'So you burgle houses and commit robbery, yet you didn't mention the boarding house so as not to get the proprietor in trouble?'

'Yes.'

'Did you give your correct name?'

'Yes, I did.'

'Why not a false one if you are so professional?'

'I don't know.'

'I suggest you never went to Sunwin House to buy clothes, just as you never robbed a man at a cashpoint in Brook Street.'

'No, I did.'

'So, at this boarding house, you showered and changed?'

'Yes.'

'What did you do with your dirty clothes?'

'I put them in the Sunwin House bag and threw them in a bin on The Grove.'

'So, you returned to the town centre?'

'Yes.'

'And then?'

'I went to a pub called the White Horse.'

'And was it there you allege you saw Amy Hodges?'

'Yes.'

'So, you were clean and shaven?'

'Yes, I was.'

'Not like Amy described you later at the house, dirty, smelly and unshaven?'

'No.'

'You see, you are making this up, I suggest, to try and explain how a smart nineteen-year-old virgin would be picked up by a forty-five-year-old dishevelled man?'

'That's not true. Everything happened as I have said.'

'And, in the pub, you say you caught her eye?'

'Yes, and she smiled at me.'

'How many girls were with her?'

'About three or four.'

'So, they would all see you chatting her up?'

'Yes. Whether they would tell you the truth about it is anyone's guess.'

'Did you buy her a drink?'

'I can't remember.'

'Because that would involve you, if you were polite, asking them if they wanted a drink. After all, you now had over two hundred pounds in cash in your pocket.'

'I can't remember if I bought a drink.'

'After all, the purpose of going to a pub is to have a drink.'

'I can't remember. I had a full pint when I went to speak to her.'

'Would they have heard your arrangement to meet her?'

'No, we did that quietly.'

'So, you took her to one side, did you, and she suggested meeting the following night at ten o'clock?'

'Yes.'

'It's fantasy, isn't it, Mr Mallinson?'

'No, it's the truth.'

'Very well. Let's move on.'

'Did you stay the night at the boarding house?'

'Yes.'

'Did you have breakfast the following morning?'

'Yes.'

'Were there any other guests present?'

'Two men, as I remember.'

'Did you talk to either man?'

'No, I keep myself to myself.'

'Really, Mr Mallinson? You have just told us that you chatted up a strange nineteen-year-old girl in a pub when you were on the run.'

'That's different.'

'And you knew the police were still looking for you?'

'Yes, I did.'

'So, what did you do on what we know was the day of the wedding?'

'I stayed indoors.'

'So, if the police came checking, they would have found you in your bedroom?'

'Yes.'

'I suggest, Mr Mallinson, all this is fantasy. Yes, you escaped, but you stayed living rough until you entered The Hollins?'

'No. That's not right.'

'Well, let's move on. You stayed indoors until about ten o'clock in the evening?'

'Yes.'

'You didn't go out to eat?'

'Oh, yes, I did. I went to an Indian in Ilkley.'

'And did you pay cash?'

'Yes.'

'So, then you got a taxi you say?'

'Yes, from Brook Street.'

'So, you walked back into the centre of Ilkley?'

'Yes, I did.'

'Which taxi did you take?'

'I think it was Ilkley Taxis.'

'A taxi to The Hollins, Middleton, Ilkley, at about ten o'clock?'

'Yes.'

'Well, that can be checked. And when you got to the house, you paid the driver?'

'Yes.'

'How much?'

'I can't remember.'

'When did you buy your knife?'

'The day after, when I knew they were after me for the murders.'

'But I thought you always carried a knife for your own protection?'

'Normally, yes.'

'So, what were you intending to do with the knife?'

'Protect myself.'

'From the police?'

'Maybe.'

'You see, Mr Mallinson, I suggest you acquired that knife, identical to the one used in at least two of the murders, after you escaped from custody, because you knew the police were after you.'

'No, it was after a search was on for me for the murders.'

'And you had it with you when you entered The Hollins?'

'No.'

'Where did you get it?'

'At Morton's in Ilkley with the money I stole.'

'I suggest you stole it from a hardware shop after you escaped from Bingley Magistrates' Court.'

'No.'

Turnbull turned to Jasper and whispered: 'Come with me,

outside.'

Once outside the courtroom, Turnbull said: 'Dave, I want you to get evidence of five things ASAP. One, no robbery reported of £300 from Brook Street, as Mallinson suggested. Barclays will be able to confirm whether or not someone withdrew £300 from the cashpoint. Two, check Ilkley Taxis to see if they took a fare to The Hollins at about ten o'clock on the night of the wedding. Three, check with Morton's to see if they sold a Bowie or sheath knife on the 25th or 26th. Four, find out where you can buy handcuffs and, five, check on 42 The Crescent.'

'Will do,' said Jasper as he headed out of the courthouse. Turnbull went back into court where Beecroft was continuing to cross-examine Mallinson.

'So, it would be unusual not to have a knife on you after your escape?' asked Beecroft.

'Yes.'

'You took it, I again suggest, to The Hollins.'

'No, I didn't buy it 'til the day after.'

'So, it's a coincidence, is it, that the knife used to murder Mr and Mrs Hodges was of the exact proportions of the one in your possession on your arrest?'

'Yes, it is. All sheath knives are that shape.'

'When and how did you acquire the handcuffs, Mr Mallinson?'

'I never did acquire any handcuffs.'

'You see, I suggest that as a professional burglar, you knew where to acquire handcuffs. They are part of your stock-in-trade in case you disturb a householder.'

'No, I never carry handcuffs.'

'I suggest you went to the house, having watched the family go out, and you set about looking for valuables, but you were disturbed by the family returning earlier than you expected.'

'No. I went in at the invitation of Amy.'

'And had unprotected sex with her?'

'Yes.'

'Did she say she wasn't using any contraceptive device nor taking the pill?'

'No, she didn't.'

'So, she risked pregnancy?'

'I suppose so. Yes.'

'It's just fantasy, isn't it, Mr Mallinson?'

'No, it's not.'

'How did Amy get handcuff marks on her wrists?'

'I've no idea. She must've self-harmed.'

'To corroborate her story?'

'Yes, I suppose.'

'And when you left her, was she quite happy?'

'Yes.'

'And then you went back to the boarding house and slept the night?'

'Yes.'

'The truth is that you went on the run once you left the house, having committed three murders and the robbery of the watch and necklace from the person of Amelia Hodges.'

'Not true. I did nothing wrong.'

'Then why not just give yourself up?'

'Because I didn't think you'd believe me.'

'Nor do we, Mr Mallinson.'

'Mr Mallinson, you say, as I understand it, that this perfectly respectable nineteen-year-old virgin agreed to have sex with you, an escaped criminal, at what was, in effect, your first meeting?'

'Yes, I do.'

'Without protection?'

'Yes.'

'And you are forty-five years old and she is nineteen?'

'Yes.'

'And that it was totally by chance that the same night, an unknown man arrived at the house soon after you had left and murdered three members of her family. Quite a coincidence, would you agree?'

'Yes.'

'And arising out of that coincidence, you have been wrongly charged with three murders?'

'Yes.'

'And the girl, Amy, has quite maliciously said on oath that you are responsible for the murders when she knows that is a lie?'

'Yes.'

'And she has fabricated injuries to her wrists to substantiate her story?'

'Yes.'

'So, you have been extremely unfortunate.'

'Yes.'

'From a good night out, when you chanced upon an attractive girl to have sex with you, you have ended up charged with three murders and a rape?'

'Yes.'

'When you aren't guilty of any?'

'Correct.'

'And, even worse for you, when you were first interviewed, you unwisely lied by saying you never went to the house?'

'Yes.'

'Why lie? Why not say, from the outset, that you had sex and left?'

'Because I thought you'd blame me for the murders which is what has happened.'

'Why would you think that you would be blamed for the murders? Is it because you realise that your story is incapable of belief?'

'Well, as you say, I'm the victim of circumstances.'

'And not only that but, as you have said, you have chanced to have sex with an inveterate liar who knows perfectly well that her sex with you was consensual and that you never murdered her family. Why do you think she would do that, because the effect of her lies is that the true culprit is free, at large, able to murder again?'

'That's true.'

'So, you are the victim of appalling injustice?'

'Yes, I am. I didn't murder any of them, or rape her.'

'And a further coincidence, I suggest, which wrongly points to you as the culprit, at the time of your arrest, as you have said, you had with you a Bowie-type knife with an identical size of blade to that used to murder the three victims?'

'Yes.'

'So, you are the victim of at least four coincidences which quite wrongly point to you as the killer?'

'I didn't murder anyone. It's true I went to the house, but I drank champagne and ate cheese. Are those the hallmarks of a killer?'

'Well, Mr Mallinson, it is I who asks the questions, not you. But, this once, I will give you an answer. They are the hallmarks of an extremely dangerous psychopathic killer.'

'Well, that's what you say.'

'I suggest to you, Mr Mallinson, that you are the killer. You entered that house via the unlocked patio window, with the intention of burglary and you were surprised by the arrival of the three members of the family. And to deal with the crisis, in the heat of the moment, you murdered them.'

'Then why didn't I murder the girl as well?'

There was a murmur throughout the court at that answer. *That's the best point the defence have,* thought Turnbull.

'Only you know the answer to that question, Mr Mallinson. But whatever the answer, she has been able to have an artist's impression drawn which is the spitting image of you. Do you agree?'

'If you say so.'

'Just look, please, at the artist's impression.'

Mallinson examined a copy of the artist's impression in the bundle in front of him in the witness box. The jurors were asked to look at the copy in their bundles.

'You agree, do you not, that you are looking at an artist's impression of you?'

'Yes.'

'So, not only has Amy falsely accused you of rape and triple murder, but she has created an almost exact likeness of you while knowing perfectly well that you are not the killer?'

'Yes.'

'How wicked is that?'

'Very. She knows our sex was by agreement but she daren't admit it.'

'So, according to you, she lied to save face?'

'Yes.'

'Out of embarrassment?'

'Yes.'

'But who survives for her to face when embarrassed? Her parents and her brother are dead. What would telling the truth matter?'

'Her friends, her relatives would think less of her.'

'And that is the best you can come up with as a motive for her lies?'

'It's the truth.'

'So, in the terror of the moment, finding her parents and her brother dead, she has instinctively, out of self-preservation, lied to save face?'

'Yes.'

'And created injuries to back up her story?'

'Yes.'

'The truth, Mr Mallinson, as you will know it, is that you slaughtered three members of the Hodges family and raped the fourth.'

'No.'

'My Lord, I have no more questions,' said Beecroft.

Turnbull thought that the cross-examination had been good.

The judge addressed Mr Mountfield: 'Have you any questions in re-examination, Mr Mountfield?'

'Yes please, My Lord, if I may. Mr Mallinson, why escape from the Magistrates' Court?'

'I get claustrophobia. I regret it now. I probably wouldn't have got a custodial sentence.'

'No more questions,' said Mountfield.

'Well, we'll adjourn until 10:30 a.m. tomorrow. The jury retired, then the judge. Turnbull went to meet Beecroft, Oldroyd and Gibson in the conference room.

Jasper arrived back at court after making his enquiries and joined the others in the conference room.

Turnbull approached Beecroft: 'Your cross-examination was excellent. It laid him bare for the liar he is.'

'Don't count your chickens,' said Beecroft. 'The fat lady hasn't sung yet. Have you anything new to tell me?'

'Well,' said Jasper. 'I've been out making enquiries with a

view to you possibly calling evidence in rebuttal.'

'Good,' said Beecroft. 'What have you found?'

'Firstly,' said Jasper. 'There was no robbery of £300 reported. I checked with Barclays Bank as to whether there were any withdrawals of £300 from their cashpoint that afternoon. There were seven, but we haven't had time to check whether any of the seven was in fact robbed.

'Secondly, Ilkley Taxis say they had no fare to The Hollins at about ten o'clock on the evening of the 26th.

'Thirdly, there are seven shops in Ilkley which sell knives. The most likely would be Morton's in the centre of town. They didn't sell a bowie or sheath knife, but they are checking their stock to see if one was stolen from a display.

'Thanks,' said Beecroft. 'We can apply to call evidence in rebuttal of the fact there was no robbery reported as being evidence ex improviso, i.e. that we could not have anticipated his evidence of the robbery. However, I think the defence may admit this evidence to save us calling it.

'As to the taxi evidence, I think we should have anticipated that, so I doubt the judge will let us call that evidence, but we'll see. Anything else?'

'Number 42 The Crescent is a boarding house in Ilkley, run by Mrs Brewis.'

'Thanks,' said Beecroft. 'We'll wait to see what other surprises are in store.'

Chapter 19

The court reassembled the following morning. Turnbull wondered who else the defence were calling.

Mr Mountfield stood and said: 'I call Edna Brewis.' Turnbull wondered if this was the landlady of the boarding house. He looked to the back of the court and saw Captain Clarke grinning at him. *God,* thought Turnbull, *Clarke is running this show, producing witnesses to try and get a not guilty verdict.*

Edna Brewis entered the witness box. She looked, to Turnbull, to be in her fifties. Her hair was grey, swept up in a bun and held in place by a scarf. She wore thick, but imposing, spectacles. She held her handbag closely in front of her. Turnbull noticed she was not wearing a wedding ring. She was overweight and wearing flat shoes.

She took the oath and faced Mr Mountfield.

'Your full name, madam?'

'I'm Edna Mary Brewis of 42 The Crescent, Ilkley.'

'And your occupation?'

'I'm a landlady. I've a lodging house in a nice part of Ilkley. I've had it for years. I used to run it with my husband, Ernest, but he died three years ago. I now run it with my daughter, Elsie. Very reasonable my rates are, if you ever want to try it.'

The jury laughed. *She's creating a good impression,* thought Turnbull, *the jury like her, she's one of them.*

'How do you record reservations?'

'In my reservations book.'

'Do you have your reservations book with you?'

'Oh yes, I've brought it specially. It's my life is this book. You're not going to confiscate it, are you? I can't do without it, you see.'

'No, madam, have no fear of that,' said Mountfield.

Mountfield addressed the judge: 'My Lord, may the witness refresh her memory from her reservations book?'

The judge addressed Mr Beecroft: 'Any objections, Mr Beecroft?'

'No, My Lord,' replied Beecroft. 'But I would like an opportunity to examine it before I cross-examine the witness, as will the jury.'

'Do you wish time now, or when Mr Mountfield has finished his examination in chief?'

'I would prefer it, My Lord, when Mr Mountfield has finished his examination in chief.'

'Very well,' said the judge. 'Yes, Mr Mountfield, you may continue examining your witness.'

'Thank you, My Lord. Mrs Brewis, how many rooms do you have available for rent?'

'Only four, sir, and very nice they are too.'

Some members of the jury smiled.

'Mrs Brewis, please would you look at your entries for September 25th and 26th of this year and read them out.'

'Yes, sir. I had three guests those nights. Mr Pottinger. Very smart gentleman, a rep for a company that sells stickers, so he tells me. Ever so charming is our Mr Pottinger.'

'Who else?'

'Mr Overend, sir. He's an elderly gentleman. Very quiet. He always likes to have the same room, number five on the first floor. Not too many steps.'

'Do you know what he does for a living?'

'A retired gentleman, sir.'

'And who was the third?'

'Here he is, sir, Mr Mallinson.' She pointed to the dock.

There was a murmur in the court and everyone took in the significance of the evidence. The 26th was the night of the wedding.

Turnbull whispered to Jasper: 'This is about his appearance, when he entered The Hollins, to rebut Amy's description of him and of the time he left.'

'Mrs Brewis, did you see an artist's impression on television?'

'Oh, yes, and very good it was too. I knew straight away it was our Mr Mallinson.'

'Which room did he have?'

'Number six, sir, on the second floor. A small room, but very nice. It has some of my grandma's prints on the wall. Very good they are too.'

'How did he pay?'

'Cash, forty pounds per night for two nights. Very reasonable if you ask me, seeing as Ilkley is so smart these days.'

'So, he paid for two nights?'

'Yes, the 25th and 26th in room six.'

'Did he come down for breakfast on the 26th?'

'Oh, yes. Very smart and tidy was our Mr Mallinson. He looked as though he took care with his appearance, if you know what I mean. He likes his aftershave does our Mr Mallinson.'

'So, he was well-shaven on the morning of the 26th?'

'Oh, yes, sir. He was very spick and span was our Mr Mallinson.'

'I have no more questions of this witness, My Lord. Is this a convenient moment for the break my learned friend, Mr Beecroft, requested?'

'Yes, I think so,' said the judge. 'How long do you want, Mr Beecroft?'

'Ideally overnight, My Lord,' replied Beecroft. 'I don't

know, at this moment, how long this particular piece of string is.'

'No, I quite understand, Mr Beecroft.'

'The judge turned first to the witness and said: 'We're going to adjourn now until tomorrow morning at 10:30. In the meantime, you must appreciate you are still in the witness box, so no talking please to anyone, and I mean anyone, overnight about your evidence. Do you understand?'

'Yes, My Lord,' said Mrs Brewis. 'But I can talk about anything else?'

'Oh, yes,' said the judge who then turned to the jury and said: '10:30 a.m. tomorrow please and remember, no talking outside your own number. You may go now.'

The jury retired. The court clerk called: 'All rise.' Everyone stood and the judge retired.

Turnbull and Jasper made to leave court, but Turnbull stopped alongside Captain Clarke.

'I know what you're about, Captain Clarke,' said Turnbull. 'You have set up this witness and Hardcastle to try to discredit Amy Hodges. How many more? All to try to keep Mallinson in circulation to carry out dirty tricks for you. I am surprised you are prepared to stoop so low. Is 42 The Crescent one of your safe houses?'

'I don't know what you're talking about, Mr Turnbull,' said Clarke. 'I'm just here as an interested observer.' And he smiled.

Turnbull and Jasper left court and went to the conference room. Beecroft and Oldroyd were already there with Myles Gibson. Turnbull and Jasper sat.

'Sorry we're late,' said Turnbull.

'What's your impression so far?' Beecroft asked Turnbull.

'Well, sir, I think this witness has been set up to give this evidence to rebut Amy's evidence that on the 26th September, Mallinson was dirty, unshaven and smelt badly of BO, having been living rough since his escape from Bingley Magistrates' Court. Also, that he didn't leave until 6:00 a.m.'

'I agree,' said Beecroft. 'But who set her up?'

'I think it was Captain Clarke who I told you about. He's been sitting in court throughout the trial, almost giving the impression of orchestrating the defence. I think Mrs Brewis runs a safe house for MI5. She's a classic for that. Having a few guests as a front, but in the pockets of MI5 whenever wanted.'

'So, you think that her evidence is fantasy?' asked Beecroft. 'That she occasionally has guests as a front, but her house is kept by MI5 as a safe house?'

'Yes, sir, I do. And I think they've got at Hardcastle. We need to look at this book. Maybe we can prove it.'

No sooner had Turnbull said that, there was a knock on the door and the defence solicitor walked in with the book.

Beecroft thanked him and opened the book at the relevant page.

Beecroft said: 'I would like to study this with Oldroyd for an hour and then we will pass it to you to do the same. We'll meet here in two hours. Do you agree?'

Turnbull and Jasper retired to the police room.

'What do you think, Dave?' asked Turnbull.

'Well, sir, firstly we should check on the two other people she said were staying that night. Secondly, we should look to see if Mallinson's name has been added in the book on those two dates as an afterthought. Thirdly, we need to check earlier and later dates in the book. We could take one or two at random and check their authenticity. We also need to check whether Mallinson has stayed there in the past.'

'I agree,' said Turnbull. 'Will you and Jane check out

Messrs Pottinger and Overend? Find out if they stayed and whether they saw Mallinson and what they do. See if they are known to us. Try and find out where they vote and what jobs, if any, they have, etcetera, etcetera.

'Will do,' said Jasper.

Chapter 20

Jasper collected the addresses for the two men and he and Jane started checking on each one. Jasper took Pottinger and Jane took Overend.

Pottinger, Jasper found, was registered as a voter in Harrogate, which was only eight miles or so away from Ilkley. He wondered why Pottinger would be staying alone at a guesthouse in Ilkley when his home was so nearby?

Jasper rang Pottinger's telephone number. A lady answered.

'Is that Mrs Pottinger?' he asked.

'Yes, love,' she replied.

'Can I speak to your husband, please?'

'Yes, love, he's in the garden. Shall I say who's calling?'

'Yes, Detective Sergeant Jasper of the Bradford Homicide Squad.

'Oh,' said Mrs Pottinger sounding somewhat surprised.

Mr Pottinger came to the phone: 'Yes?' he said.

'Mr Pottinger, I am Detective Sergeant Dave Jasper of the Bradford Homicide Squad. Your name has come up in the investigation into the murders of the Hodges family in Ilkley. I trust you have read or heard about the murders?'

'Oh, yes, but in what connection has my name come up?'

'Well, it's alleged you stayed the nights of the 25th and 26th September this year at a guest house at 42 The Crescent, Ilkley. Is that correct?'

'Yes, that's right.'

'Why stay there when you only live a few miles away in Harrogate?'

'I went to a party and rather than drink and drive, I stayed in Ilkley.'

'Why alone? Why wasn't your wife with you?'

'It wasn't that sort of party.'

'And why stay two nights and not just one?'

'Look, what is this? The third degree?'

'No, Mr Pottinger, it's a murder investigation and doing acts tending and intended to pervert the course of justice is a very serious offence. Are you sure you stayed there at 42 The Crescent?'

'Well, I think so, yes.'

'Who else was there?'

'Two other people appeared at breakfast.'

'Alone or together?'

'Alone.'

'Would you recognise either or both?'

'I don't know. I never spoke to them.'

'Do you watch television?'

'Yes, of course.'

'Have you seen anyone on TV you recognise as staying at 42 The Crescent?'

'No.'

'Mr Pottinger, do you know a Captain Clarke?'

'No, why? Should I?'

'I don't know. You tell me. Do you work?'

'No, I'm retired.'

'What sort of work did you do? What was your occupation?'

'I was in the security services.'

Wow, thought Turnbull, *I wonder how many people in Yorkshire just happened to have worked for the security services?*

'So, you didn't work for a company selling stickers?'

'No.'

'Did you tell Mrs Brewis that that's what you did for a living?'

'Certainly not.'

'Are you sure you don't know Captain Clarke?'

'No, I don't know him.'

'I think you do, Mr Pottinger, he's with MI5.'

'No, I don't know him.'

'When you stayed at 42 The Crescent, did the other two men come in for breakfast both days?'

'That, I can't remember.'

'Was this the first time you stayed at 42 The Crescent?'

'Yes.'

'So, quite out of the blue, you stayed there by yourself for two nights on the 25th and 26th September?'

'Yes.'

'Thank you, Mr Pottinger, we may be in touch with you again.'

* * *

Jane Rowley's task was to find Mr Overend, if he existed. Jane eventually traced him to an address in Leeds. *How strange,* she thought, *staying in Ilkley when you live half an hour away. Hadn't Jasper told her that Pottinger did the same? Strange, unless they were at the same party. But why stay for two nights?*

Jane managed to speak to Mr Overend who confirmed that he had stayed at 42 The Crescent for two nights.

'Why two nights?' asked Jane.

'I went to a party.'

'Alone?'

'Yes.'

'Was there a Mr Pottinger at the party?'

'That, I don't know.'

'Whose party was it?'

'John Charles.'

'Of what address?'

'The Pines on The Drive in Ilkley.'

'Was it a celebration?'

'Yes, I think so.'

'What of?'

'I can't remember.'

'Why on your own?'

'It was only me who was invited.'

'Why?'

'That, I don't know.'

'What do you do for a living?'

'I am now retired. I was in the security services.'

'So, you know Mr Pottinger?'

'No, not really.'

'Well, it so happens that he also was in the security services.'

'Really?'

'And he also says he stayed and number 42.'

'Really?'

'And was the mysterious John Charles also in the security services?'

'Yes.'

'Do you know Captain Clarke of MI5?'

'No.'

'Would you recognise the third man who was staying at the guest house?'

'No.'

'Do you realise that doing acts tending and intended to pervert the course of justice is a criminal offence?'

'Yes, of course.'

'Thank you, Mr Overend.'

* * *

Turnbull and Jasper met Beecroft and Oldroyd in the conference room at court, as arranged, taking Jane Rowley with them.

Beecroft said: 'Oldroyd and I have been studying Mrs Brewis' reservations book. It's very interesting. You'll hear about what we've found in our cross-examination of this witness, the mysterious widow, Edna Brewis. What have you two found?'

Jasper and Jane related their discoveries.

'Very interesting. Both ex-security services. Both going alone to the party of a third ex-security man and both staying two nights, not one, when both live nearby. Fishy,' said Turnbull.

'The problem is,' said Beecroft. 'I can't see how we can get these facts in evidence and that Mrs Brewis' evidence is all false. We have closed the prosecution case. The only way we could get it in is to apply to the judge to call evidence in rebuttal. But rebuttal of what? Mrs Brewis' evidence suggesting an MI5 conspiracy to discredit Amy Hodges' evidence that the murderer is Mallinson. The jury would probably think it is a far-fetched idea and even if we succeeded in an application to call the evidence, it could backfire on us. The judge himself could then apply to call Clarke, if he's still here, and he would simply deny it.

'So, I think all we can do for now is cross-examine Mrs Brewis on her so-called reservations book and on her evidence generally.'

'I accept that,' said Turnbull. 'We'll just have to see how it goes.'

'Right,' said Beecroft. 'See you tomorrow.'

141

* * *

The court reassembled at 10:30 a.m. the following day. Mrs Brewis entered the witness box and Beecroft stood to cross-examine her.

'Mrs Brewis, this man you say was Mallinson paid for two nights on the 25th and 26th September?'

'Yes.'

'And he paid cash in advance?'

'Yes.'

'Did he sleep there on the night of the 25th?'

'That, I can't say.'

'But surely you would have noticed whether or not his bed had been slept in?'

'I can't remember.'

'Or, if he came down for breakfast the following morning?'

'I can't remember.'

'You said earlier that he came down for breakfast looking smart.'

'I can't remember.'

'So, the last time you saw him for certain was on the 25th September when he paid you cash? You cannot say whether you even saw him on the 26th?'

'That's correct.'

'Did you give him a receipt?'

'Yes.'

'Is there a carbon copy of that?'

'No.'

'Why not?'

'I don't keep copies.'

'How then do you do your accounts? Surely you have to

142

show your receipt book with your accounts?'

'You're getting me confused.'

'Did you see him after he paid you on the 25th?'

'I can't remember.'

'Did you ever see an artist's impression on television either late evening on the 26th September or on the morning of the 27th?'

'Can't say I did.'

'Did he sign a register?'

'No.'

'Do you not require your guests to sign a register?'

'Not always.'

'Surely it is an established practise in the tourist industry to require guests to sign a register?'

'If you say so.'

'Mrs Brewis, have you ever stayed at an hotel without signing a register?'

'When we go abroad, I don't.'

'But in the UK?'

'I can't remember.'

'Mrs Brewis, do you know a Captain Clarke of MI5?'

'Can't say I do.'

'Did you know, Mrs Brewis, that Mallinson was on the run, having broken out of Bingley Magistrates' Court?'

'No.'

'Well, it was publicised.'

'No, I didn't hear.'

'And yet you say he booked in using his correct name?'

'Yes.'

'Did the police come to your house at any time to check who was staying?'

'No.'

'Regarding Mallinson, did you notice any physical injury on him?'

'No.'

'Well, his leg was bleeding from a deep cut, Mrs Brewis.'

'No, I didn't notice.'

'You see, when he came to you, he came straight from an escape from custody.'

'Well, if you say so.'

'But he had no luggage.'

'That, I don't know.'

'Well, he can't have had, Mrs Brewis. Yet you say he was clean and smart and shaven?'

'Yes, when I saw him.'

'And he had on him sufficient cash to pay in advance. How much did you say? Eighty pounds?'

'Yes.'

'Mrs Brewis, who has put you up to giving this evidence?'

'I resent your implication. He's here, in the book.'

'You could have put that in at any time.'

'I suppose so.'

'And do you say that he stayed before then?'

'I can't remember.'

'Well you seemed to give that impression. You referred to him as *our Mr Mallinson*.'

'No, he only stayed the once.'

'Thank you, Mrs Brewis,' said Beecroft, who sat.

'Any re-examination, Mr Mountfield?' asked the judge.

'No, My Lord,' replied Mountfield.

'Thank you, Mrs Brewis,' said the judge. 'Mr Mountfield, are you calling any more witnesses?'

'No, My Lord,' said Mountfield.

'Beecroft stood: 'My Lord, the defence make certain

admissions of fact at this stage of evidence.

'Firstly, that no report was made of a robbery from the Barclays cashpoint on Brook Street, Ilkley, on the afternoon of the 25th.

'Secondly, that no fare from Ilkley to The Hollins, is recorded with Ilkley Taxis at or about 10:00 p.m. on the night of the 25th.

'Thirdly, Mortons did not sell a Bowie knife on the 21st of September.'

'That is correct is it, Mr Mountfield?' asked the judge.

'Yes, My Lord,' replied Mountfield.

'Very well, we will adjourn there until 10:00 a.m. tomorrow,' said the judge. 'The timetable tomorrow, members of the jury, is that we will hear speeches from counsel, first by prosecuting counsel and then by defence counsel. And then I will sum up the case for you. I expect you to be going out to consider your verdict early in the day after tomorrow.'

Turnbull and Jasper retired and went to Jacob's Well for a beer. Beecroft hadn't wanted another meeting and Turnbull was glad of that. Jane Rowley and Jonathan Crawford joined them. Turnbull bought a round of drinks.

'Well done all of you. Now the jury has to do some work for a change.'

Chapter 21

The court reassembled at 10:00 a.m. Prosecuting Counsel stood to make his final address.

'May it please your Lordship. Members of the jury, let us together look critically at Mr Mallinson's version of events.

'He accepts he is a professional burglar. He uses a device to pick locks and burgles people's houses. He admitted six burglaries when arrested. Compare that image with that in the witness box. The urban, coiffured man in a suit, white shirt and tie. Don't be deceived by that appearance.

'He finds himself in custody because he triggered an alarm, when committing a house burglary, and the police were waiting for him. Careless of him, he says. If he hadn't been caught, no doubt he would have continued burgling houses with the inherent risk of confronting a householder.

'He signs for his effects at the custody sergeant's desk. He then, using his skills as a burglar, silently breaks a window in the holding room and slips out.

'What he did thereafter was to go on the run. But he has to discredit Amy's description of him as dirty, smelly and unshaven, when he entered her bedroom.

'So, he makes up, because there is no record of such a crime, that he robbed a man of three hundred pounds in Brook Street in the centre of Ilkley. And he uses that money, so he says, to pay for accommodation in the very vicinity of his robbery in Ilkley.

'He has to say he looked smart when he alleges he met Amy, so he fabricates that he buys a change of clothes and toiletries from Sunwin House, very near to where he committed the robbery, and then goes to Mrs Brewis' boarding house.

'He tells Mrs Brewis, so it is said, his correct name. He does not sign a register, which means there is no signature to compare with that obtained by the custody sergeant.

'At some point he either steals or, according to his version, buys a Bowie-type of knife or a sheath knife from Morton's in Ilkley. Yet, they have no record of such a sale.

'Notwithstanding the fact he was on the run, he alleges he went to a public house where Amy Hodges, an attractive nineteen-year-old virgin, not on the pill and without any form of contraception, invites this forty-five-year-old back to her house quite obviously, on his version, for sex. She, according to him, doesn't care about the risk of pregnancy.

'You heard from Amy and Georgina Stewart that no such meeting took place in the White Horse pub in Ilkley.

'He then says that, the following night, he got a taxi from Ilkley town centre to The Hollins. No such fare was recorded by Ilkley Taxis. He then enters the house, having been let in by Amy, and then drinks champagne, eats cheese and has unprotected sex with this nineteen-year-old, after which he says goodbye and goes back to his lodgings.

'So far, so good. But then, horror of horrors, a strange man, not Mallinson, enters the house and is interrupted by the return of the family. Amy discovers the bodies after the intruder has left and decides, quite gratuitously, to allege Mallinson is the murderer, thereby ensuring the true murderer is never caught.

'Not only that, she fakes marks on her wrists which, by chance, match exactly those which would be made by hand-cuffs and alleges to the police that the man with whom she made love consensually was, in fact, the murderer and indeed the robber of her mother's jewellery.

'Meanwhile, Mallinson sees on television that he is wanted

for three murders which he knows he never committed. He panics and goes on the run, carrying with him a knife of exactly the proportions of that used in at least two of the murders. What an extraordinary coincidence. Of all the knives in the world, he picks one exactly the same as that used by the true murderer. How unlucky is that?

'He gets as far as Lofthouse, but he is seen by DCI Turnbull and DS Jasper from the police helicopter. He hides in a barn and is caught by the armed response unit. He is taken to Bradford Police HQ where, under questioning, he makes no mention of staying at Mrs Brewis' guest house and denies ever going to The Hollins.

'Then his blood sample is taken, his fingerprints are taken and his teeth marks are recorded which give the lie to his account of never having been at The Hollins.

'Now he has to change his tack. Even Arthur Mallinson can't dispute scientific findings, no fewer than three lots: his finger prints on the champagne bottle, his teeth marks in the cheese, his blood on the nightdress. The girl had been so keen on sex, she was happy to have it, without contraception, with a forty-five-year-old man whose leg was bleeding.

'When confronted with this evidence, Mallinson takes the only tack he can. He can't deny drinking champagne, he can't deny he ate the cheese. His only route consistent with innocence is to say Amy consented to sex and he left before the true murderer arrived who, by sheer coincidence, comes into the house to burgle, presumably whilst Amy is still upstairs in bed and who is surprised by the arrival of the three members of the family who he then murders.

'So, Amy finds three members of her family have been savagely murdered. Then, in this distraught state, she decides, according to him, to lie. This poor girl, whose family has been slaughtered, presumably sits down and thinks *I know, I will blame the murders on the man whom I met in the pub, say he raped me to save face and the embarrassment of having to admit I had consensual sex and say he murdered the three.*

'Then she thinks, to corroborate her account, *I will make up that he handcuffed me.* And so, she quite deliberately cuts her wrists, simulating exactly the marks of handcuffs which Professor Talbot recognises as handcuff marks. How clever is that? To make up the fact she was handcuffed and then to create the marks which exactly accord with the marks she would have received if she had been genuinely handcuffed.

'It is just not possible, members of the jury. And, if she wasn't raped, why allege she was? She could just as easily say she saw the attacker without mentioning rape.

'The defence in this case is sheer fantasy, thought up by a desperate man who is a killer.

'Amy's evidence of rape is compelling. The fact of rape is corroborated by the handcuff marks and, to an extent, by her extreme distress, although I accept that distress is consistent with the distress of finding the three closest members of her family murdered.

'You may ask *What do the prosecution say about Mrs Brewis?*

'Firstly, we say her evidence is not believable, not credible.

'Where did this man on the run get the eighty pounds to pay Mrs Brewis? Not from a robbery that was never reported. And he would know that the police were after him for burglary and escape from lawful custody; his name would be circulated as a wanted man once he escaped. Would he then check into a boarding house using his correct name, this experienced house burglar?

'And how did he get to look, as Mrs Brewis put it, spick and span? He had been in the same clothes for days. He had, on his escape, no razor or shaving cream and none would be provided at the guest house, so he has to make up the Sunwin House purchases and the robbery to explain how he paid for them.

'And did he stay there? Mrs Brewis couldn't say whether his bed had been slept in, or whether he had breakfast. No sign in the witness box of the other two men who slept there the night.

'According to her, this stranger, whom she refers to inappropriately as *our Mr Mallinson,* arrives unannounced at her boarding house where there just happens to be a free room.

'Mrs Brewis can't remember whether Mallinson had any luggage. Whereas, on his version, he had by then acquired a Sunwin House bag, but nothing else.

'So, what then? Mrs Brewis records that he booked for two nights but never asks him to sign the register. How odd is that? Or is it because the defence know that they have his genuine signature on the custody sheet which could be compared with any signature purporting to be that of Mallinson in the boarding house register?

'No, Mrs Brewis' evidence is not credible. Forces are afoot behind this case that we do not know about. We cannot speculate as to how or why. Our *Mr Mallinson* staying was a complete fabrication.

'What of the evidence of Mr Patterson? Unfortunately, it is a fact of life that there are cranks in this world who, to gain fame, will admit crimes they never committed in the knowledge that they will never be prosecuted. Twenty-four hours of notoriety is what they seek. Rather pathetic individuals who read newspaper reports and cull from them the basic facts which they then put forward as the basis of their false confession. They fall down on the detail which the police have deliberately withheld from the Press. Which is precisely what happened here.

'When Patterson was first interviewed, he said he had gained entry by smashing the front door. Wrong. The front door was not smashed. The intruder gained entry somehow, without force. Entry, as we know from the CCTV recording, via the patio door.

'According to Patterson's first interview, he killed all three in the sitting room. Wrong. Gordon Hodges was murdered on the stairs. Amelia Hodges was murdered in her bedroom and David was murdered in his bedroom as he lay sleeping. Patterson left no fingerprints in the house to support his account.

'The knife he used, he says, was a carving knife from his home. He handed that knife over to the police and it has been examined by Professor Talbot. He's an expert on wounds. The wounds to Mr and Mrs Hodges, he said, before he had even seen Mallinson's knife, were caused by a Bowie or sheath knife of exactly the type and dimensions of the knife Mallinson had in his possession on arrest. Patterson's carving knife could not have killed either Gordon or Amelia Hodges.

'What of, say the defence, the evidence of Fred Hardcastle? Mr Hardcastle, you may think, is a professional handler of stolen goods. A fence, if you like, who should think himself very lucky not to be prosecuted for receiving the stolen watch and necklace. But he is a police informer who informs on what he hears from the underworld.

'When first asked about who sold him the jewellery, he said it was Mallinson. Since then he has been got at, ladies and gentlemen. Now he says he thinks it was Patterson, the man you will remember who gave a completely false description of the murders to the police and who never even mentioned he had robbed Amelia Hodges of any jewellery when interviewed by the police. He now says he smashed down the door to gain entry, yet the family were having a drink in the sitting room when he confronted and killed them.

'Members of the jury, the man who robbed Amelia Hodges of her watch and necklace was Arthur Mallinson. He then went to Skipton where he sold the items to obtain cash and then headed north, sleeping overnight in the rain shelter on the fourth hole at Masham Golf Club. Thereafter, when disturbed by the green-keeper, he continued on the run.

'He would not, you may think, have been seen were it not for the bright-eyed Detective Sergeant Jasper in the police helicopter.

'The armed response unit are called and Mallinson is found hiding under straw in a barn. He is taken to Bradford Police Headquarters where he denies ever having been to The Hollins. The rest you know.

'Ladies and gentlemen, keep your eyes on the ball and your minds fixed on the evidence of Amy Hodges. What a plucky, intelligent, nineteen-year-old young woman she is who was out, with friends, the night before the wedding. It is inconceivable she would be picked up by a forty-five-year-old man like Mallinson and have unprotected sex. She never met Mallinson, as confirmed by Georgina Stewart. Her account of rape is corroborated by the marks you may think were uniquely caused by handcuffs.

'Remember her appearance, as described by the Weatherheads, as she stood in the doorway to the marquee, describing how her family had been slaughtered and she had been raped. She was distraught beyond belief.

'And remember her face in this trial when she was accused of lying and of having consensual sex with Mallinson. The look of sheer horror on her face at the prospect of sex with this smelly, dirty, forty-five-year-old murderer of her family.

'Where Mallinson got the handcuffs, we will never know. You may think it was part of his house-burgling kit. A knife, handcuffs, lock opening device, all in case of emergency. Such a man knows where to get his equipment.

'Mallinson, let there be no doubt, murdered Gordon, Amelia and David Hodges, leaving tell-tale marks of having done so on Amy's nightdress when he raped her.

'Only one verdict is possible in this case, members of the jury, and that is guilty on all four counts of the indictment.'

* * *

The judge thanked Mr Beecroft and called on Mr Mountfield to make his final address.

Mountfield stood. There was a hush as he put his papers on his small lectern mounted on the court bench. He turned to face the jury. Behind him was the court window facing towards the Victoria Hotel opposite.

'Ladies and gentlemen of the jury, let us examine together, bit by bit, the prosecution case just in the same way as my learned friend for the prosecution has done with the defence case.

'Someone committed three dreadful murders. That, of course, is obvious. The defence team concede three murders were committed. But what of the fourth count of rape? It doesn't fit into this pattern of behaviour. It's rather like a round peg in a square hole. The two don't fit.

'Mallinson is a professional burglar. He carries with him, if intent on burglary, all the tools of the trade. Would they not include gloves if he is as expert as it seems he was?

'On the 22nd September 2008, he was caught by tripping a beam whilst committing a burglary. Careless. He admitted six other burglaries, for which he had not been caught, committed in the same manner with the sophisticated lock-picking device. Those burglaries he would ask to be taken into consideration when sentenced. His method was to enter a well-to-do house, when the occupants were out, by picking a lock, stealing jewellery or cash and then exiting as quickly as possible. His sole purpose was theft of high value, portable items.

'Yet this burglar of The Hollins, Ilkley, if the prosecution are to be believed, enters this house without gloves, without any of his burgling paraphernalia, the paraphernalia of a professional burglar. And he gets into the house without picking the lock. How did he do that? He had no gloves. The Crown's case is that he got in via the patio door, yet there are no fingerprints on the outside of the door. Odd. And it can only be opened from the outside when there is a gap into which to get fingers to slide it. Otherwise, if fully closed, even it isn't locked it can't be opened from the outside. And if someone tried, surely they would leave finger marks if not wearing gloves.

'So, how did Mallinson get into the house?' The obvious answer is that he was let in. There could, in common sense, be no other way.

'The other strange thing about the prosecution case is that Amy was left alive. That fact is the elephant in the room which the prosecution has avoided tackling throughout this case.

'If Mallinson is the ruthless, pathological killer, which the prosecution allege, why did he not kill Amy?

'Not only that, he has no disguise. So, Amy is able to reproduce that artist's impression which is the spitting image of Mallinson.

'If he is the killer, would he leave alive a bright, young nineteen-year-old who is able to produce such an excellent artist's impression of him? He would have murdered her as well.

'Life has no value to this murderer. And no doubt he would know that if he murdered three, four wouldn't make much, if any, difference to his sentence.

'Yet, this professional burglar, if the prosecution is to be believed, enters the house without disguise and without gloves. He drinks champagne, leaving his fingerprints on the bottle. He eats cheese from the fridge, leaving his teeth marks on the cheese, marks which can be traced and, indeed, have been traced to him.

'And then he leaves his blood on Amy's nightdress. Three tell-tale signs which scientifically prove he entered this house. What happened to this man's professionalism? This man who had never previously been caught. It, on the prosecution version of events, does not make sense.

'You will ask yourselves, is there another possible explanation? It is not for the defence to prove anything. Our purpose is to cast doubt on the prosecution version of events. And if you have any reasonable doubt, that must lead to verdicts of not guilty because the prosecution would not have satisfied you so that you are sure of guilt.

'So, what other explanation is there? Well, straight off, one possible explanation for the patio window opening without fingerprints on the outside, is that the window was opened from the inside which, of course, is easy to do because that is meant to be the way the patio door or patio window is opened. And you have the CCTV recording to show that happening. You cannot see whether there is a person on the other side of the glass inside the house.

'What you can see, however, is how easily the window is opened. If it was unlocked and someone was trying to open the window from the outside, but the window was fully shut, it could not be opened or, at the very least, it would be difficult.

'If an attempt was made to open it, surely there would have been smudge marks on the outside of the window. There were none.

'So, the chances are, submit the defence, that this window was opened from the inside. The only person who could have opened it was Amy. She was the only person in the house.

'It is here that the prosecution version of events begins to fall apart. I am afraid, from the prosecution point of view, this evidence makes life difficult because why open a window from the inside to a man standing on the outside? Answer, because you have invited him. Once you have reached that conclusion, you must ask why has she invited him and when?

'The only opportunity to invite him was in the public house on the night before the wedding when Amy was in such an establishment, the White Horse in Ilkley, with her friends.

'The prosecution says it is inherently unlikely that an attractive nineteen-year-old girl would invite a forty-five-year-old man to her house after the wedding. I suggest it might depend on his appearance. If Mallinson is right, by then he was in a new suit of clothes bought from Sunwin House together with shaving equipment. We submit he would have looked as he did in the witness box. We agree he is forty-five, but is he that unattractive? That is for you to decide. But the door was opened from the inside to someone she let in and Mallinson says it was him and, on the prosecution version of events, it couldn't have been anyone else.

'Then he drinks champagne and eats cheese, leaving obvious clues that he has been in the marquee and house. He then admits having sex with Amy. There is no damage to her private parts. Of course, we accept that submission is not the same as consent. But there is nothing inconsistent in her private parts with consensual sex. It is said the sex was unprotected.

Mallinson had a vasectomy in the past and so there was no danger of an unwanted pregnancy. Whether she knew that, we don't know because neither Amy nor Mallinson was asked.

'And then, according to him, he leaves. The only evidence capable of corroborating her account of rape is the handcuff marks. They, of course, are not in her private parts region but, says Professor Talbot, they are consistent with handcuffs.

'But where, on the prosecution case, did Mallinson get the handcuffs? It is suggested he stole them from the Keighley police. No evidence has been called that any were missing after Mallinson's escape. No evidence has been called that he could have bought them from a hardware shop like Morton's. Have any of you ever seen handcuffs for sale in a hardware shop, or anywhere else for that matter?

'It is alright for the prosecution to say the marks are consistent with handcuffs when there is a complete absence of evidence as to where he would have got them. It's rather like saying: *It is a gunshot wound, but there is no evidence an accused had access to a gun.*

'The defence has no idea where Amy got the marks. All we can say is that they are not from handcuffs which Mallinson had access to, nor were they on him at his arrest. Knife yes, handcuffs no. Why, if he kept the tell-tale knife, did he not keep the tell-tale handcuffs?

'It is true Mallinson lied when arrested, but lies are not definitive of guilt. It is human nature to lie when confronted with a frightening allegation. He went on the run when he saw his picture on television. He knew he'd been in the house and that he could be blamed for the murders, which is precisely what happened. But he, on his version, told the truth in the second interview.

'The crucial fact here is that he did not kill Amy. That fact means, we submit, that he did not commit the murders. The scientific evidence of fingerprints and teeth marks simply confirm the he was in the house, nothing more.

'The blood on Amy's nightdress and feet is consistent with her going to her mother and father's bodies, as any daughter would, to check on whether they were dead. The fact he was let into the house, which is the most sensible conclusion, is indicative of consent. The willingness to let himself not only be seen, but traced by fingerprints and teeth marks suggests he was there by her invitation.

'At the very least, you must have doubt about the truthfulness of Amy's account which lies at the heart of the prosecution case. Once you have reached that conclusion, how sure can you be that Mallinson did not leave before the murders were committed, particularly when you knew that Patterson had admitted committing them?

'However, the defence do not have to prove that Patterson committed them. The sole purpose of his evidence was to cast doubt upon the prosecution case that it was Mallinson who committed them.

'We submit you must have doubt upon the rape count and once you have reached that position, the other three counts of murder fall like a stack of cards.

'We submit you cannot be sure of Mallinson's guilt and that your only possible verdicts are ones of not guilty on each count.

Chapter 22

The judge began his summing up at 2:15 p.m.

'Members of the jury, you have heard all the evidence you are going to hear. There will be no more evidence. Each side decides what evidence it is going to call. And you have heard excellent and succinct speeches from counsel, each extolling the points in the evidence upon which they rely. Now it is my task to sum the case up for you.

'You and I have very difference functions, as will have become apparent to you during the trial. I am the judge of the law and procedure. I give rulings on matters of law which you must follow, but you, and you alone, are the judges of the facts. It is for you, and you alone, to decide whether the prosecution has proved that Mallinson is responsible for all, or any, of these offences. It is you who must make all decisions of fact as to who is truthful and who is untruthful, or indeed who is truthful at one point in his or her evidence and untruthful at another.

'For the sake of completeness, notwithstanding the fact that it is conceded that three offences of murder were committed, it is my duty to define the offence of murder for you. Murder is the unlawful killing of another with intent to kill or cause grievous bodily harm.

'Here, two victims were repeatedly stabbed in the chest causing death either at the time, or soon after. David's throat was cut and he died at the time, or soon after. It is accepted by the defence that each of the three was murdered.

'The sole issue for you to decide, in counts one to three, is whether you are satisfied so that you are sure that Mallinson was the murderer.

'I turn to the offence of rape. Rape is committed by someone who has sexual intercourse with a woman who, at the time, does not consent, or who is reckless as to whether or not she consents.

'There is no dispute that Mallinson had sexual intercourse with Amy.

'The question for you to decide, in count four, is whether you are satisfied so that you are sure Amy did not consent, or alternatively whether Mallinson was reckless, not caring whether Amy consented or not.

'The burden of proving Amy did not consent is throughout on the prosecution.

'Submission to sex is not the same as consent. Submission through fear is not consent. You should look for some evidence from an independent source, confirming Amy's account that she did not consent, before convicting Mallinson of rape.

'The evidence relied on by the prosecution as corroboration is, firstly, the evidence of the marks on Amy's wrists. I direct you that the evidence of marks to Amy's wrists is capable of corroborating Amy's account of rape. Whether they do is a matter for you. The prosecution says the marks were made by handcuffs and that the marks are exactly consistent with those which would be made by handcuffs. The defence do not dispute this. They do, however, dispute that Mallinson applied any handcuffs and they remind you that none have been recovered from him, nor have any laces. A suggestion was made to Amy that she made these marks in order to make her account of rape more credible. What you make of that is a matter entirely for you.

'Secondly, the defendant's lies to the police, when interviewed, are capable of corroborating Amy's account of rape. It is for you to decide whether you are sure he lied because he knew he was guilty. If you are sure of that, the lies are capable of confirming Amy's account and you are entitled to convict him of rape. If you are less than sure that he lied because he is guilty, but think it possible he lied out of panic rather than guilt, then you should disregard those lies as corroboration of her evidence.

'Her distress, when seen by the Weatherheads, the doctors and the police, is not capable of being corroboration of her allegation of rape as it is equally consistent with a reaction to the deaths of her family members.

'If you are sure Amy was telling the truth, you are entitled to convict of rape even if you were unsure that the marks and the lies confirmed what she said. But you must be wary of doing so.

'There are four counts in this indictment. You must consider each separately, although you may think they stand or fall together.'

The judge then turned to the evidence and reminded the jury of the salient parts of the evidence from both prosecution and the defence witnesses.

'Finally,' he said. 'Members of the jury, when you retire, you must strive to reach verdicts upon which you are all agreed. If a time arises when I can accept from you verdicts upon which you are not all agreed, I will call you back into court and give you a further direction.

'Now, when the bailiffs have been sworn, will you retire to consider your verdicts. If you need any help as to the evidence which has been given, do not hesitate to send a message to me and I will, in court, give you what assistance I can.'

The jury bailiffs were sworn to keep the jury in some quiet and convenient place and not to speak to them unless to ask if they are agreed upon their verdicts. The jury retired, taking with them their bundles.

Turnbull and Jasper left court and returned to headquarters.

'What do you think, Dave?' asked Turnbull.

'Well, if the jury apply their common sense, Mallinson will be convicted. There are, however, gaps in our case which the defence exploited. How he got into the house is a tricky point. If the jury think Amy may have let Mallinson into the house, then that will have a knock-on effect,' said Jasper.

'I'll ring to find out how Amy is,' said Turnbull. He picked up the phone and dialled Amy's aunt's house. Pleasantries were exchanged and he asked Violet how Amy was.

'She's okay,' said Violet. 'When we get the verdicts, we're taking her to Spain for a week.'

'Give her my best,' said Turnbull. 'She's a plucky lass. I'll let you know the verdicts as soon as we get them.'

Turnbull left a message for Myles Gibson to ring him at police headquarters as soon as the jury had verdicts. His office was only a few minutes' walk away from court.

By 4:30 p.m. there were still no verdicts and the members of the jury were sent home by the judge with the usual warning not to talk about the case, not to do any research on the internet and not to watch or read any news reports about the case. In bygone days, jurors were confined in an hotel, but that rule was abandoned for cost reasons.

Turnbull and Jasper invited the team to the pub where Turnbull bought the drinks.

'Well done all of you,' said Turnbull. 'It's now in the lap of the Gods.'

Chapter 23

The following morning, at ten o'clock, the jury came in. The judge entered the courtroom and bowed first to counsel and then to the jury.

'Please will you now retire again and continue your deliberations,' said the judge to the jury, who then filed out of court. The judge also retired.

Turnbull and Jasper went to the police room where they waited and waited for the verdicts, getting more and more anxious as time passed. Jane Rowley's enquiries about Patterson had led to nought. He had not falsely confessed to any other crimes.

At 4:00 p.m. the judge called counsel back into court.

He addressed counsel: 'Mr Beecroft, Mr Mountfield, the jury has now been out for approximately eight hours. I propose, subject to anything you may say, to give them a majority direction. Have either of you any objection?'

'No, My Lord,' replied counsel in turn.

'Very well. Jury back please,' said the judge to the clerk.

The jury filed back into court.

The clerk stood and said: 'Will the jury foreman please stand.'

A plump man, who Turnbull had guessed would be the foreman, stood.

The clerk asked the foreman: 'Has the jury reached verdicts upon which they are all agreed?'

'No, My Lord,' said the jury foreman.

'Thank you, Mr Foreman,' said the judge. 'Please sit down. Sufficient time has now elapsed whereby I can accept from you verdicts upon which not all of you are agreed, namely on which at least ten of you are agreed.

'So please retire again and strive to reach verdicts upon which you are all agreed but, if that is not possible, I am now able to receive verdicts from you upon which at least ten of you are agreed; ten to two, eleven to one or unanimous verdicts. Is that clear?'

The members of the jury all nodded.

The jury retired again. The judge retired and Turnbull and Jasper went to meet the prosecution team, in their conference room.

'Well, well,' said Beecroft. 'It may be just one or two who are holding out. I can't believe the split is any greater than that, but we have no way of knowing. I suspect the problem is mode of entry and, for some, Patterson's evidence. I assume that if the jury can't agree, you will want a retrial?'

'Yes, so far as the police are concerned,' said Turnbull.

'The same with the CPS,' said Gibson.

'Mallinson would be kept in custody until retrial,' said Beecroft. 'But it would mean that poor girl having to give evidence again but that, I'm afraid, can't be helped. By then, the two other girls from the pub would, I assume, be available to give evidence.'

'Let's hope it doesn't come to that,' said Turnbull. He and Jasper then retired to the police room and read the day's papers. Jane came across from headquarters to find out what was happening. There was nothing to report.

At 4:00 p.m. the judge sent the jury home, yet again, until ten o'clock the following morning.

'Let's hope no one on the jury has been got at. I'll believe anything of that Captain Clarke. He's devious in the extreme,' said Turnbull to Jasper as they walked out of court, only to see

Clarke as he was leaving. He smiled at Turnbull.

'Did we miss anything?' Jasper asked Turnbull.

'I can't think of anything. Every case has the odd point of difficulty. Here there are several and if one or two jurors are strong characters and latch on to defence points or ones they think of themselves, who knows what can happen.' Turnbull was thinking of the film *The Twelve Angry Men* starring Henry Fonda. 'Try not to think about it. Go home, have a nice evening and I'll see you tomorrow.'

Turnbull decided that he'd had enough for the day and would go home early for a change. He drove back to Idle. Helen was at home.

'You're early,' said Helen who was watching a cookery programme she'd recorded. 'I'll make you a cuppa. Sit down and put your feet up.'

Turnbull was so grateful to have a wife who understood the rigours of a policeman's life. He knew so many whose marriages had broken down because of the unsocial hours of work. He and Helen had never had any children, but Helen seemed to have accepted the situation without demur. She worked part-time at the local library and seemed content with her lot in life.

Turnbull drank his tea and dozed off, wondering what the jury's verdicts would be.

* * *

At ten o'clock the following morning, the judge came into court in the absence of the jury. He addressed counsel: 'I have received from the jury a note which discloses the state of their deliberations. In accordance with established practise, I do not propose to disclose it to you, but simply to tell the jury to continue to deliberate.'

Counsel agreed.

Turnbull knew that it was not appropriate, in accordance with established law, for the judge to say in open court how the jury was divided. 'I think,' he said to Jasper. 'That means they are near to verdicts, maybe three standing out. Otherwise, he would have asked the foreman if he thought that, with extra time, verdicts would be possible. I think this note is a good sign.'

The jury was brought back into court and the judge addressed them: 'Members of the jury, I have received your note, for which I thank you. At present, I propose to say nothing to you save will you now retire again and continue to deliberate. The jury retired, as did the judge. Turnbull and Jasper went back to the police room.

'This is excruciating,' said Jasper.

'It's worse for the jury,' said Turnbull. 'They've been out now for more than twelve hours.'

Another hour passed and then an usher appeared at the door. 'The judge has asked for counsel,' he said. Turnbull and Jasper returned to court.

The judge entered the courtroom: 'Mr Beecroft, Mr Mountfield, I am disposed to give to the jury what is known as a Watson Direction. Have either of you any observations to make?'

'No, My Lord,' said Beecroft and Mountfield in turn.

'Very well,' said the judge. 'Jury back please.'

The jury filed back into court. The clerk said: 'Will the foreman please stand.' The portly foreman stood.

'Mr Foreman,' said the clerk. 'Has the jury reached verdicts upon which at least ten of them are agreed?'

No, My Lord,' said the foreman.

'Thank you, please sit,' said the clerk.

The judge then addressed the jury: 'Members of the jury, each of you has taken an oath to return verdicts according to the evidence. No one must be false to that oath, but you have a duty, not only as individuals but collectively. That is the strength of the jury system.

'Each of you takes into the jury box with you your individual experience and wisdom. Your task is to pool that experience and wisdom. You do that by giving your own views and listening to the views of others. There must, necessarily, be discussion, argument and give and take within the scope of your oath. That is the way in which agreement is reached.

'If, unhappily, ten of you cannot reach agreement, you must say so. Will you now retire once more to continue with your deliberations.'

Once again, the jury went out and Turnbull and Jasper retired to the police room.

'What that boiled down to was whoever is holding out, see sense and follow the rest,' said Turnbull.

'Why didn't he say so?' asked Jasper.

'Because he can't. That would sound too much like badgering them,' said Turnbull.

At the lunchtime break, the police team went to a local Indian restaurant for lunch. Turnbull treated them all, thanking them for their hard work. After lunch, he and Jasper returned to court and went to the police room for a coffee.

At 3:00 p.m. the usher came to the door. 'We have verdicts,' he said.

'Thank God,' said Turnbull as he and Jasper returned to the courtroom.

There was a solemn hush as the jury came in. They pointedly avoided looking at the dock. *Is that a tell-tale sign?* Turnbull wondered. The judge then came into court.

The clerk addressed the jury: 'Will the foreman please stand.' The foreman stood.

'Mr Foreman, has the jury reached verdicts on which at least ten of your number are agreed?'

'Yes,' replied the foreman.

'On count one, alleging murder of Gordon Hodges, do the jury find the defendant guilty or not guilty?'

'Guilty,' said the foreman.

Clapping erupted from the public gallery. The judge waited for it to subside and then said: 'If there is a repeat of that behaviour, I will cause the court to be cleared.'

'Is that a unanimous verdict or by a majority?' asked the clerk once quiet was restored.

'By a majority.'

'How many agreed and how many dissented?'

'Ten agreed, two dissented.'

'On count two, alleging murder of Amelia Hodges, do the jury find the defendant guilty or not guilty?'

'Guilty,' said the foreman.

'Is that a unanimous verdict or by a majority?' asked the clerk once quiet was restored.

'By a majority.'

'How many agreed and how many dissented?'

'Ten agreed, two dissented.'

'On count three, alleging murder of David Hodges, do the jury find the defendant guilty or not guilty?'

'Guilty,' said the foreman.

'Is that a unanimous verdict or by a majority?' asked the clerk.

'By a majority.'

'How many agreed and how many dissented?'

'Ten agreed, two dissented.'

'On count four, alleging rape of Amy Hodges, do the jury find the defendant guilty or not guilty?'

'Guilty,' said the foreman.

Again, there was a loud murmur of approval from the public gallery.

'Is that a unanimous verdict or by a majority?' asked the clerk.

'By a majority.'

'How many agreed and how many dissented?'

'Ten agreed, two dissented.'

'Thank you, Mr Foreman, you may sit down.

The judge addressed the jury: 'Thank you for your services in this case which must have been a harrowing experience for you. You are excused from jury service for fifteen years.

'I will sentence the defendant at ten 'clock tomorrow morning. You may return for that if you wish.'

'All rise,' said the clerk. The judge bowed and retired.

Turnbull and Jasper waited for things to quieten down. They didn't want a press interview. Some officers in charge of cases loved the glory. Turnbull did not. His job was over and he was happy to take a back seat. He and Jasper walked to the door of the court. Captain Clarke was waiting there at the door. He was no longer smiling.

'Well done, Mr Turnbull,' he said. 'You got the result you wanted.'

'No thanks to you,' said Turnbull. 'You did everything you could to try and achieve the opposite result when you knew perfectly well that Mallinson was guilty.'

Clarke did not respond but said: 'Here is my *White Envelope*. Will you see that the judge gets it?'

'I will,' said Turnbull. 'Will you excuse me?' He and Jasper went to the conference room where Beecroft and Oldroyd were packing up their papers.

'At least Mallinson will be out of circulation for a while. We'll see you tomorrow,' said Beecroft.

'Well done, by the way,' said Turnbull.

'And you,' replied Beecroft.

Turnbull and Jasper then headed for the police room where Turnbull rang Amy: 'He's been convicted on all four counts. He will be sentenced tomorrow.'

'Good,' said Amy. 'Well done, Mr Turnbull, thank you for letting me know. I'll be going as soon as possible.'

'Good luck, Amy, take care,' said Turnbull.

'Thank you, 'bye.'

Turnbull then went to the court clerk's office where he found her at her desk recording the verdicts on the court log.

'I have what's known as a *White Envelope* for the judge's eyes only. It's from Captain Clarke of MI5. I assure you that it's authentic.'

'Thanks,' said the clerk. 'I'll see the judge gets it. Well done, by the way. A nasty piece of work that Mallinson.'

'Thanks,' said Turnbull. 'See you tomorrow.'

Turnbull and Jasper went back to headquarters where they were met by the rest of the team.

Jasper said: 'It all seems a bit of an anti-climax.'

Turnbull wondered what was in the *White Envelope*?

Chapter 24

The following morning, the court reassembled at ten o'clock. Three of the jury had returned to hear the judge's sentencing remarks. The court was packed.

'All rise,' said the clerk. And the judge came into court. The press sat at the ready.

The case was called on. Mallinson came into court, handcuffed and escorted by three burly prison officers. *They're not taking any chances,* thought Turnbull.

The judge addressed Mr Beecroft: 'Anything known, Mr Beecroft?'

'No, My Lord, the defendant is a man without any previous convictions.'

'Thank you,' said the judge. 'Mr Mountfield, do you wish to say anything?'

'No, My Lord, thank you.'

The judge then addressed Mallinson: 'Stand up please. You have been convicted by the jury of three counts of murder and one of rape. You slaughtered three members of a highly-respected and loving family. You then raped the one member of the family whom you had left alive. These were truly appalling crimes for which you have shown no remorse. There is no mitigation. However, I take into account all that I now know about you.'

Turnbull thought that this was an oblique reference to the *White Envelope.*

The judge continued: 'The sentence on counts one to three is one of life imprisonment. I recommend that you serve a minimum of eighteen years imprisonment.

'On count four, I sentence you to twelve years imprisonment to run concurrently.

'Take him down.'

The press rushed for the door.

Turnbull was shocked at the eighteen years recommendation. He had expected far more. *It must,* he thought, *have been the contents of the White Envelope which brought the sentence down.*

Turnbull and Jasper went to meet Beecroft and Oldroyd in the conference room. Turnbull was well aware that only he knew about the *White Envelope. How,* he wondered, *could he advise Beecroft on whether the prosecution should appeal the sentence as being unduly lenient?* He was in a classic cleft stick.

'What do you think?' Beecroft asked him.

'Well, it's a lenient sentence, but I think it unlikely that the parole board will ever let Mallinson see the light of day.'

'I agree,' said Beecroft. 'Something brought the sentence down. I saw you talking to Captain Clarke during the trial. I suspect our Mr Mallinson was a more complex character than I thought. I suspect Clarke may have sent the judge a *White Envelope.*'

'I couldn't possibly comment,' said Turnbull, smiling.

'That's enough for me,' said Beecroft. 'The press will bleat about the sentencing, but I don't believe Mr Mallinson will ever taste freedom. I advise against appealing the sentence. Many thanks for all your hard work.'

'And thanks to you both,' said Turnbull.

Turnbull and Jasper shook hands with Beecroft and Oldroyd and left court.

'Fancy a pint, Dave?' said Turnbull.

'I thought you'd never ask,' said Jasper.